**Ony**

A novel

By

Donna L Campbell

# Part One

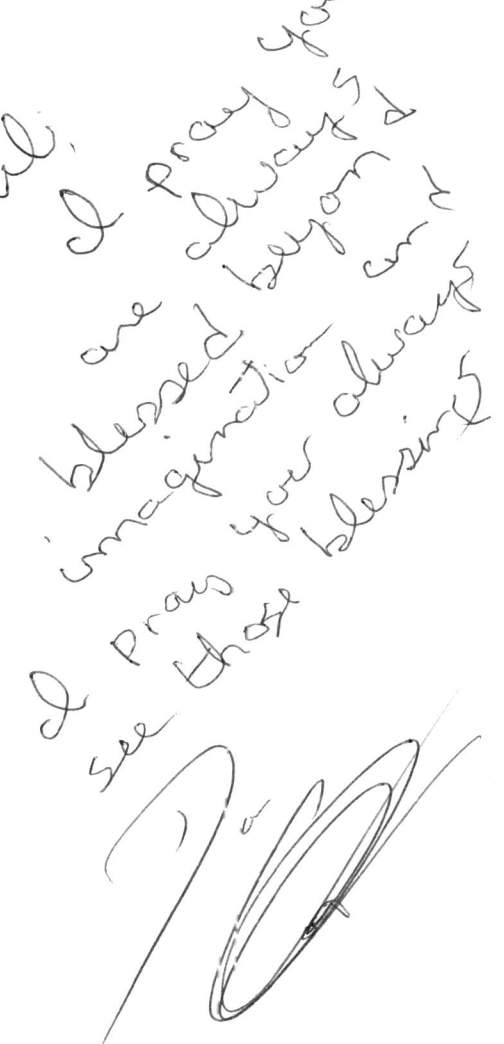

Ali,
I pray you are always blessed beyond imagination and I pray you always see those blessings

# 1

Luke stepped out of the ranch house and walked with sure paces off the porch, down the three steps and then twenty feet to the fence. He knew these steps without thought. He also knew Caleb, the teenaged son of his housekeeper, followed behind him at the insistence of the motherly woman. It had bothered him at first that Melba couldn't trust his safety, but he let it go after six months of trying to convince her he could walk around his own ranch without worry. She worried enough for the both of them and he let her have this concession, he pretended not to know Caleb was there. He let Caleb do the important job of protecting him. It made the boy feel better and it made Melba feel better. He thought deep down it made him feel a little better too.

He had been blind for three years now, the longest and shortest of times. He often woke from dreams wondering why everything was so dark, then he would remember. There were times when he tried to remember Melinda's face and found he couldn't picture her. Or someone would describe something to him and he would not be able to recall yellow or the difference between green and blue. Sometimes he would expect Melinda to be in the room waiting for him to come in from his long day, but of course, she wasn't there. He would reach out in the night to fold his arm around her and find cold emptiness instead. He had lost her the same day he had lost his sight. He would have given much more to save her, to have her there. But of course he hadn't been offered the choice.

He had actually required Caleb once when he had tripped on a log and come very close to a silent but deadly snake. He'd had no idea it was there, preparing to strike him. Caleb had said very quietly but sternly "Mr. Logan! Stay very still! Don't move!"

Luke heard the urgency and the fear in that voice and he stayed still. Fear gripped him he had no idea what danger lurked, he just knew it was very close. He could do nothing to stop it. Then the sound of something hitting the ground less than a foot in front of him made the urge to move desperate, but Luke remained perfectly frozen.

Caleb touched his hand gently with his own trembling hand. His voice was almost teary he was only fourteen, tall, skinny and in that chasm between boyhood and manhood. "It was a snake, Mr. Logan, right behind the log. I got him with my knife."

Luke got to his feet, pulled the boy close to him for a moment before he patted him on the back. "Well done Caleb!" He spoke with much more bravado than he actually felt. He hoped the boy couldn't sense his shaking as the adrenaline rush let go of his body. "What kind was it? Should we make some snake stew for dinner tonight?"

"A Mohave! They're really deadly, He could have gotten us. I don't think I'd have the stomach to eat it."

Luke cut short his daily walk and took the boy back to the main house, so he could be relieved of his clandestine duties for the day. Luke considered making his own furtive plan to leave again but the snake had pointed out a weakness in him that he had not wanted to consider. He decided working around the house might be a better plan.

This day Luke's hand found the fence post and balanced lightly on it as a guide. He strode along past Harvey as he tamed a horse in the small pen, past Lee as he did repairs to the bunk house, and toward the large pasture of cattle. The smell of grass, manure, feed and sweat met him as he neared the large meadow. He listened to two of his men, Charlie and a new guy, Jed as Charlie explained which of the cattle would have to be branded. The conversation went suddenly silent as Luke neared them and Charlie cleared his throat and said "Mr. Logan! Sir, I was just telling Jed here that we're gonna have to wrangle those two over there and get them branded, we missed them last week when we were branding the young ones."

Luke assumed he pointed somewhere into the large herd grazing in the field. "Good, keep up the good work." He walked away from the two men staying along the fence. He listened as the men began to acknowledge Caleb behind him before the young man could silence them. He laughed to himself. He enjoyed his alone time but this was not solitude. He longed for the quiet privacy of old. It was a rare treat anymore.

He wanted to run ahead away from the fence and to the seclusion of the hills that he knew lay to the west of his land. But he couldn't trust he would know where he was without the sturdy wooden rail under his hand. Running was just a misty memory of youth. So he accepted his limitations for the tenth time that day. He accepted them begrudgingly. There were few things he wouldn't try, but walking lost on his huge property could result in his death, so he stayed to the fence, and kept his position in his mind always. This was as private as his life could be now, people lingering, watching and worrying always close at hand.

He was twenty three years old, the owner of a large and prosperous ranch, he was a widower and even a hero to some. He had fought for the Union. He had watched his brother and father die fighting for the Union. He had dozens of employees, all loyal and respectful. He was a pillar of his community. Yet, he couldn't get on his horse and ride out alone.

He began now making his way toward the house. He would have to find his main man, Ike, to help him finish the payroll, so the many people who depended on him could get their monthly salary. He should have had more to do than spend two hours strolling his land, but his men did a good job. Ike, Harvey and the rest were reliable. They showed him complete respect and they fired anyone that didn't. Luke felt he earned the respect. He stayed as involved as he could. He was on a horse when they moved the cattle. He was the decision maker. Nothing happened without his say so. Not a man was hired that Luke didn't speak to. He ran his business well.

Luke's hand came suddenly to a broken piece of fence. He reached ahead and took tentative steps searching for the next piece. He made a note of where he was so he could send some men to fix this, this was the southern edge of the property about two miles east of the grazing pasture they were currently using. He wondered why it was broken and how it had been broken. He felt along the broken fence and found a several broken posts fallen and haphazard. He continued forward knowing he couldn't look helpless in front of Caleb. He could hear the boy's held breath as Caleb tried to decide what action to take. Luke didn't want him to feel the need to run to his rescue it was just a few feet of broken fence. Luke walked, tripped over a fallen post, and got up again. He walked past the railings for what he guessed was maybe twenty feet before he found solid fence again. As his hand touched the solid wood, Caleb let his breath out. Luke had to hold his laughter at the boy's nervousness to himself.

There should be no horses running free here to break a fence. Maybe someone had let their horses break through his property. He'd send someone out looking tomorrow.

Luke stopped by the bunk house and told Joe to let Ike know he was ready to meet with him in his office and continued back home. He stepped into the house to the smells of roasting meat and herbs. His stomach growled. He went to the kitchen where his robust housekeeper Melba was singing a hymn as she cooked the supper. Luke knew every inch of his home and never had an unsure step there. He went directly to the table and found the still hot bread cooling. Without asking he took the knife, which he knew Melba would have next to the loaf and cut a thick slice.

Melba pretended to be upset with him for cutting into it. "Mr. Logan! That bread is for dinner! You are not the only hungry man around here." She tutted her tongue, took the bread, spread butter onto it, set it on a plate and gave it back to him. "At least eat it like a civilized human being and sit down."

# 2

Luke sat down as she ordered him to, and ate the delicious bread. She set down a cup of milk and without thought put his hand on the cup for him. He drank the milk and thanked her. Theirs was an easy relationship. She had been the housekeeper in his home since he had been a boy. She had married Harvey, and the two had lived in a small house behind the main house and raised three sons, of whom Caleb was the youngest. She had been the mother figure in the home for most of those years. She had watched Luke, and his older brother John grow up. She had been there to see John Sr. John Jr. and Luke leave with the other men to fight in the war. She had been there when Luke had returned to his Nevada home alone. She had held him against her ample bosom as he had cried in secret. He had cried for the loss of his family and the horrors of that war to her only and just that once. She had been there when he met Melinda and when he decided he loved her and married her. She had been there when he awoke after that horrible day to find he had lost his wife and his vision. He had cried then too, once for his blindness and weeks for his lost love. She was an overprotective, loving busybody and he loved her dearly.


Luke finished his snack and went to his office to await Ike. Ike was a small half Shoshone man with dark leathery skin and long dark hair. He had a quiet voice and an even temperament that immediately gained admiration from the ranch hands he supervised. Ike had taught Luke lots of little tricks to deal with blindness, making it easier for him to navigate his home and his ranch. Apparently Ike's grandfather had been blind. Ike showed Luke how to eat his meals, how to walk without shuffling and groping, how to listen to sounds to find walls and trees nearby. He taught him countless little helps to make his life manageable. Luke depended on his foreman a great deal.

The quiet man entered the room and sat beside Luke at the desk. As he started sorting the papers to finish payroll, Luke told him about the broken fence.

"Hmm, I'll get Carl and Frank to go look at it, and fix it and they can check for anything unusual at the same time."

I think I'll ride out there with them in the morning." Luke said. He imagined his foreman looking up at him in surprise then lowering his head back to the papers.

"Mmhmm" was all Ike said on the subject and the two men got to work to prepare the paperwork for the trip to the bank on Thursday.

# 3

Early the next morning Carl arrived at the house with Frank and an extra horse. "Good morning sir." He said with a little shyness.

Luke took the man's arm and followed his careful steps to a large horse. Carl tried to help him on but Luke got onto his horse with practiced grace. Bessie was Luke's faithful beautiful chestnut steed. She was calm but loved to run. Luke loved to go riding with people and upset them all by encouraging her to race faster and faster away from the group. She somehow sensed this man's vulnerability, she was as gentle with him as if he were a child but she would nip at someone else trying to climb onto her back. She had for the last few years reluctantly let others saddle her but she would only let them lead her to her beloved master.

Carl and Frank talked very little, being around their boss made them somewhat diffident. They were both average of the sort of man that worked for Double Jay Ranch. They were uneducated, hard-working, tough men from hard backgrounds. Both had fought in the war. Neither was married. Frank had been wandering the country when Ike found him and offered him work. Carl had lost his farm to the bank after his return from the war and had been hired when he came looking for work. The stories were not un-common. While men had fought for the Union, the Union had not cared what happened to homes, farms, and families. Many had come home to find they had to start their lives over.

Luke tried to engage the men in conversation. They answered in short sentences. Talking made it easier to follow. Though Bessie knew the way, it at least made Luke feel better. By the end of the short ride the men were a little more at ease with their boss. Both realized he was friendly and humble. Neither really knew how to deal with his disability, but that was nothing new to Luke.

The Nevada sun was already warming the ground when they found the twenty foot area of broken fence. The men got off the horses and led them to an unbroken section to be tied up to the post. Luke listened to the men as the unloaded the travois of wood and whatever else they carried. He stepped to the broken fence and began to feel the posts to see if any were salvageable. What was useable he moved to his right. The posts he found too broken he moved further away to the left. He was sweating by the time he finished.

"Thanks Mr. Logan. I uh wondered what good you would be here, but I guess I was wrong." Carl said bravely. "I'm sorry I guess I shouldn't say that but I really didn't know what you could to help and heck, most bosses don't do no menial work anyhow."

Luke smiled at the man in hopes of encouragement. "You're welcome Carl. Do you have any holes dug yet?"

Frank spoke up from some feet away. "Yes sir." He said a little loudly

"Great.", said Luke. He ignored the annoying habit of having people unsure of whether a blind man could hear that he was being spoken to. "I'l hold the post and you can hammer it in.

Carl picked up and carried the first post to its place, with Luke touching him lightly on the arm to follow. They put the post in the small hole. Luke held it tightly about two feet from the top, to keep it balanced as Frank or Carl pounded it with a mallet to drive it into the ground. The third man pushed the dirt at the bottom tight around it until the post stood securely n the ground. The men repeated the procedure until all the posts stood upright, then placed the cross posts in the horizontally to make the property line secure.

Harvey had suggested more than once that barbed wire would be easier, and less expensive. Luke had told him repeatedly that barbed wire would not be any more effective at showing the borders of the property and would harm animals that might come in contact with it. He didn't share that it would also impede his ability to walk his ranch since he couldn't use barbed wire as a guide under his hand.

The men finished the work when the sun was high in the sky. The position of the sun overhead and the grumbling of his stomach told Luke it was time for lunch. While Frank and Carl loaded the travois, Luke fed Bessie a carrot he had brought along and stroked her long nose, and neck. He spoke quiet little nonsense words into her ear and listened to her little sounds speak back to him. Once the travois was loaded the men climbed onto their horses and headed back to the horses' pasture. The ride was only a mile, but Luke couldn't resist the urge to run Bessie. Carl would be unable to follow him due to the load he dragged.

Luke gripped the reigns and put his legs tight along Bessie's sides, she started galloping then running. He heard the sounds of the bewildered men behind him. Carl ordered Frank to follow. Luke realized that the men thought he was on a runaway horse and urged his steed faster. The wind hit his face, freedom bloomed around him. He knew it would be short lived so he experienced it for as long as he could. Minutes later he heard the feet of another horse beside him.

"Hold on Mr. Logan! I gotcha! Whoa! Whoa!" The hooves were very close beside him now and he felt Frank's hand take the reigns as Luke loosened his legs on Bessie's sides so she would slow down. Frank took the reins away from Luke and led the horse and man back to the pasture they had past. The joy and freedom of the morning was gone now and Luke was shamed and treated like a child. Frank was smart to remain silent on the walk back, because, had he said one chiding thing, Luke may have fired him. He hated being reminded of his disability, as if he didn't know it was there. He hated not being trusted to know his own abilities. He hated not being thought of as an equal or a man.

Once at the pasture, Luke got off his horse and led her to the water hole, with Frank right next to him, almost afraid to let him go. Finally the man said in a timid voice, "I'll take you to your house, Joe can take care of the horses for us."

Luke faced Frank and kept his voice as even as possible but cool steel came out of his mouth as he spoke. "I don't need help to go to my own house. You could have ridden with me instead of treating me like a child." He turned around and walked as confidently as possible to the house. He was angry and he felt shamed and belittled. He tried to tell himself that Frank meant well, but he didn't feel like listening. He stopped at the pump in front of the house and washed his face, hands and neck of the grime from the hard work. He let the coolness of the water lower his temperature. By the time he walked into the house his temperament had improved a little as well.

# 4

Today was the day they moved the herd to new pasture. It was one of Luke's favorite parts of ranch life. It took most of the ranch hands and all day to move the large herd the ten miles from the north pasture to the south pasture. They all rode steering the cows and bulls along the path. He had participated in the herding from the time he was very young. He and his brother John would ride near the front of the group with their Dad, making sure the cows followed behind.

He had enjoyed deep conversations with his dad during those long rides. As he grew older he enjoyed the camaraderie with the hands. Now he still enjoyed it. The air was crisp and smelled of cattle and horses. It was a smell only a cowboy could love and Luke did love it.

Bessie and he rode as one near the front leading the cattle from to the new pasture so the old one would have time to renew itself. He didn't feel blind on these journeys. He trusted Bessie to see for him. She followed Ike on his paint. Ike had refused to name his horse. He said he knew her without a name and if she knew her name, she had not chosen to share it with him.

Caleb caught up to Luke from riding further behind with his brothers. Luke loved his chances to talk with the boy. Caleb's brothers were often too busy for him. He was a sweet, big hearted boy. He longed to be thought of as an adult. Luke understood that longing, having been the younger sibling himself. He spent as much time as he could find encouraging Caleb, giving him jobs and teaching him. Caleb idolized Luke.

"I love moving the herd! Eli let me help him when one of the cows wandered too far off, and she followed me right back!" He was so excited to share his story with his hero.

"That's great Caleb. You remind me of John when he was your age. You know he was the best herder we had? Isn't that a stray cow?" Luke said and pointed past Caleb to an unknown place.

"I don't see one? Caleb said looking hard for the lost animal." Then he realized his blind friend was joking."Mr. Logan! You had me really looking. Listen, I was wondering if I could come with you to the bank Thursday."

"No, Caleb, I don't think so." Luke said quickly. He couldn't put Caleb in danger.

"Please Mr. Logan. I won't go into the bank, I just want to go to town." He begged. Caleb knew Luke had his reasons, and he even understood them. He remembered that bank trip three years ago too. But he remembered it from a child's point of view.

"I don't know Caleb. I'll talk to your Dad and see what he says." Luke thought that Caleb was probably tired of being treated like a child, but he had lots of reservations about taking the boy on the bank trip.

"Thanks." Caleb said disappointed.

# 5

After lunch Luke and Ike headed to town to the bank to get the salaries for pay. Ike carried a rifle and two guns. He had Marcus and Eli, Caleb's older brothers come along with their own guns as well. Caleb joined the trip against Luke's better judgment but was banned from entering the bank. The town of Willow Lake, Nevada, was just east of the Sierra Mountains and not very big or very dangerous, but at this time of year there were some temporary residents who stopped their westward travels for the winter before continuing to California. Because of its location the town boasted some large saloons and hotels as well as some seedier business. Luke knew first hand that dangerous things could happen here. Carrying monthly wages for over thirty people was treacherous business, and the more guns the better.

Although it had been over three years, entering the bank every month Luke still felt sick for a moment. The smells, the sounds and the atmosphere itself rekindled that horrible day for him. He pushed it back down as always, and walked into the little building. He was called over to the far window by Alfred Winters. Alfred was the owner of the bank and although he spoke in an educated manner that could be mistaken for snobbishness, he was a very compassionate man, who singlehandedly had kept many men from losing their hard earned land by extending loans as far as he could afford.

Luke and Ike went to the counter. Alfred was ready for them and took the paper work and read through it. Then went to the back room where he kept the vault. When he was ready he called Luke and Ike to the back room and they together counted out the large amount of cash and put it into the bags.

The process was long and careful and Luke found it very boring. He worked at concentration on the task throughout, yet not being able to see, he could only listen as the other two men counted. But he did listen to every word, and he packed the money into the bags so that he wouldn't think about that day. But today his mind wandered back to the day his life changed so drastically.

It had been a bright spring day, and Melinda had talked Luke into letting her come to town on the bank trip. She wanted to buy a new hat. She sat beside him on the buckboard with Ike, Mike and Harvey in the back. The sun lit her blonde curls, her green eyes twinkled with joy. She chattered about her plans for a big summer party. Luke listened with half his mind. He wished now he had truly listened to her, he couldn't recall her words just the subject. He loved this woman deeply. But He had no time for frivolity and he would discuss the party another time. He was thinking about the new ranch hand that had been drinking on the job, as well as five missing cattle over the last three months. He had so much more to think about than a party or a hat. Luke squeezed her hand in encouragement to continue talking, to say, he was listening even though he wasn't.

They entered the main street of town. The main thoroughfare was about half a mile long with businesses side by side and small alleyways and paths between leading to more businesses and then the homes of the townies. The bank lay about three quarters of the way down. It was one of the few brick structures, with glass windows and bars over them. A wooden sign above the door displayed 'Bank'. On one side of the bank was the sheriff's office, on the other was the barber. Men sat on the porches of both the other buildings but none loitered in front of the bank.

This time of year, there were a few strangers in town, and their population would grow as winter got closer. But Luke noticed the three men across the street near the Mercantile. One was tall with long brown hair hanging down to his mid arm, and a beard just as long hiding the visible portion of his face. He wore his hat low shading his eyes and making his face an enigma. The second man was small he barely reached the first man's chest, his beard was shorter but as unkempt as his greasy brown hair. The third man was just a little shorter than the first with shocking red hair and a short beard that seemed desperate to grow in. They paced, looking restless and watched the Sherriff's office closely.

Luke glanced to the porch of the Sherriff's office to see the deputy and a townie, Kyle Chance playing Checkers. He wondered if he should bring the suspicious gang to their attention, and changed his mind. It was none of his business. He didn't care for Deputy Porter. The man was smug, foolish and lazy. Let him do his own job. It wouldn't affect Luke if Porter was too absorbed in his game to pay attention to the strangers.

Luke helped Melinda down from the buckboard, while the other men disembarked from the back. "Darling," she said. "I'll be over at Sylvester's looking at the new dresses and buying that hat. I'll meet you back here before you even know I'm gone."

"Well come into the bank when you're through, we might be a while and I don't want you standing in the street alone. I should send Mike with you to the shop." Luke said.

"Please dear! I am not a wilting flower! The store is thirty feet away, I'll be fine and yes I will meet you inside the bank when I'm through." She gave him a quick peck on the cheek and was gone.

The four men entered the bank and Alfred soon called them over to him. Ike and Luke stepped into the back with Alfred. As they were packing the last of the counted bills into the bags, there was the sound of scuffle in the front. The three men rushed out of the room to see the scruffy men, large rifles in hand pointed at Will, Alfred's clerk. Will's pale face glistened with sweat and Luke could swear he was about to cry as he stared at the rifle aimed at his head.

The tall man obviously in charge bellowed in a deep voice "Give us everything you have! And you'll live!"

Luke was glad to see the only other people in the bank were Mike and Harvey. But the rifles were under the seat of the buckboard. Mike reached for his gun and the small scruffy man suddenly turned his rifle toward him with a high pitched and panicked voice he said, "Drop it! Drop it now!" The man's hands were shaking, he had a too large smile on his face that told Luke this man was on the verge of losing control.

Ike spoke in a slow voice in an attempt to calm the situation. "Mike is putting his gun down, look, so am I and we are gonna give you the money and you can be on your way." He used the same voice when taming a horse.

The small flustered man swung his rifle to Ike now, then back to Mike. "Shut up Half Breed! Everyone give me your guns and maybe you'll live!" His voice had become a faster higher pitch. He seemed ready to pull his trigger at the slightest provocation.

The medium man kept his rifle pointed at poor Will who was gathering the cash he had and putting it in a saddle bag. The tall man glared at Ike who had dropped his gun, and Mike who held his tightly in his grip.

Then suddenly everything changed. The door bells jingled and Melinda walked through the front door. Luke rushed toward her to push her back out again. The small man turned his rifle toward her and fired. Luke grabbed Melinda too late. She fell to the ground. Luke cradled her in his arms as she bled. Guns were firing all around him. He could see nothing but light and fire as he held her. He could hear only the explosions of the guns as he tried to coax her back to consciousness. Then there was a sharp pain and nothing.

Luke had woken up a couple of days later to a dark new world, in which Melinda was dead. Mike had been killed too. Ike had wounded the tall man, and killed the small one. Harvey had killed the third. Luke had done nothing but gotten shot himself, and when the bandages eventually came off, he would slowly learn to accept that he was blind. Losing his vision was nothing to him compared to losing Melinda.

It had made mourning her so much easier, as people let him alone to moping and self-pity. After a few months of it, Ike and Melba both had had enough and between them helped him move on.

"Luke! I think you're a million miles away. Come on. We're done here." Ike's voice cut through fog.

Luke stood up found Ike's Elbow and followed him silently out of the bank as he pulled himself together. They passed over the threshold of the bank and Luke wondered if it was still stained dark with Melinda's blood. He remembered the sounds of the tall man who they all found out was a bandit named Louis Peterson and called himself Big Lou, hanging. He remembered the feelings of glee as the floor opened up underneath him, and the sound of Lou's neck cracking. He remembered that fleeing joy as he realized that vengeance had not decreased his longing to have Melinda by his side.

# 6

Luke's mood had still not improved by the next day. Pay day at the Double Jay always meant a day off work with a huge dinner for everyone on the ranch. Luke had no intention of joining in this month. He didn't care about their morale today. Let them have fun. He was in the mood for solitude and he was determined to find it.

Caleb would be enjoying the party with everyone else. People expected Luke to be there, since he was the host. Melba would be too busy with the party itself.

Luke stepped out of the house as quietly as possible. The air felt cool and moist on his skin. The sounds of night still surrounded him. Cicadas sang, and Crickets chirped. The sun had not yet risen. He walked as coolly as his adrenaline pumped heart allowed him, found the fence post and continued. He thought about going to get Bessie, but that would mean going past the bunk house and possibly alerting people to his presence. So he just walked his usual path. But today he planned to go farther. By the time anyone realized he was not home, and before the party even got started he would have had hours to himself and maybe even feel good enough to join them. But right now the darkness of his mood filled him. Walking had always been a release for him. It was a time to think, to reflect and find joy.

The air became dryer and warmer as the sun rose. The chirping of crickets became the songs of birds. Luke let his mind go. He stopped thinking about where he was and just walked. After a couple of hours he regretted not bringing water or food along. Had he been able to see he could have picked some fruit or berries along the way but he only knew that he was still on his property heading west. He didn't know how close or far the fruit trees were.

More time passed as thoughts flew through Luke's mind. Why did he have to lose Melinda? Why had he let her come that day? What did he have to do to be thought of as a man? Being blind wasn't the hard part, it was that he became a lesser person. Sure the men pretended to respect him, but Luke knew they laughed behind his back. They pitied him. Melba trusted a teenaged boy more than she trusted him. He was a man! He had proved it over and over. But the others saw no proof, they saw only his blindness, the scar on his forehead and the fact that he couldn't save his wife.

Luke's hand reached the end of the fence, the southwest corner of the property. How long had it been since he had been this far? It had been before that day at the bank. He climbed onto the fence and sat by the corner post where two fences met. He was tired and hungry form the walk. He knew when he arrived home Melba would chide him for going off alone. They would treat him like a child. Ike would tell him it had been a stupid selfish thing to do. Melba would tell him all the terrible things that could have happened.

He sat on the fence, breathing taking everything in. What was beyond him? He didn't know. The landscape could have been anything. To him it was nothing, it called to be explored. He couldn't remember what was out there just beyond his knowledge. He listened. He heard the occasional sound of small animals through brush. The sun felt warm on his skin so he decided there was not a forest. His foot wanted to touch down on the forbidden land, but as angry as he had been, it had not made him foolish. Any man could get lost, a blind one more easily so. But still he sat there imagining the geography beyond him.

He listened to the wind move freely through the air. He heard a voice, feminine and desirable calling his name. "Luke." It startled him in its clarity and perfection. He had heard no one approach. Had he been so lost in his thoughts? He supposed so. He didn't recognize the voice. Who would have had the audacity to send some strange woman to fetch him miles from any of the buildings at the ranch?

"What do you want?" He shouted at the woman. He had no patience for being treated so disrespectfully.

There was no answer, no sound at all. He could sense no one at all there. Had he imagined the voice? He must have, but it didn't feel illusory.

"Is someone there?" He sounded helpless even to himself. He was vexed to have to ask, to have to depend on someone's decision to reveal themselves to him.

No one answered. No human scent greeted him. No human sound came to him.

Luke stepped down from the fence and headed back toward his home. He felt like someone was watching. But Luke knew no one was there, they couldn't conceal their presence completely for so long a time.


An hour later, he was finally feeling a little better. The walk had helped. His empty stomach and dry mouth had stopped there screaming. He thought about the voice calling his name. It had been so real. The voice had been full and seductive. It had belonged to a woman that knew more than a woman or even a man should know. That one word had held promises. Why would he dream up a voice like that?

"Luke!" Harvey's voice called out, filled with relief at finding his poor wandering boss. "What happened where have you been? We've been looking for you?"

Luke hadn't heard the horses until Harvey had called him out of his reverie. "I just thought I'd take a walk Harvey. A man has the right to walk on his own land and enjoy some time to himself!" He sounded sharp, much sharper than he'd meant to sound. But his anger was back. He resented the search for him; he resented the kind man that had found him, when he wasn't lost. Of course No one but Luke knew he wasn't lost but Luke didn't care.

"I'm sorry Luke. You should have told someone you were going out. C'mon get on my horse.'

"No, I'll walk. Luke said

"No sir, I'm real sorry, I know you're my boss, but I'm more than twenty years older than you and you're like a son to me, but more important, Melba is my wife, and she will tan my hide if I don't bring you back right now. You will get on this horse."

Luke was so surprised at the man that he let Harvey help him onto the horse and sat behind him as they made their way back to the house. It was a silent ride. Harvey knew he need go no farther in upsetting his boss who was apparently already upset.

When they got to the house Luke wanted only to go to his bedroom but Melba had other plans. She took him to the kitchen gave him a plate of food and a glass of water. The smell of the food aroused his empty stomach and thirsty mouth and Luke ate voraciously despite himself.

Melba started her tirade and kept it up throughout the meal. " We cancelled the picnic for you. No one knew where you could be. We thought maybe you had been kidnapped or worse. How dare you just go off gallivanting and leave us here to worry." She stayed on the theme until he had finished his meal then marched him to the water closet and a freshly drawn bath. "You take a bath and get cleaned up. These men deserve a party and you will be there hosting it!"

Luke did as she said. He remained silent. He washed himself, glad that at least she had allowed him this much dignity.

# 7

That night Luke lay in his large lonely bed, still awake, and offended. He needed to get past this. He had not let these issues bother him so much before. He was so tired of people treating him as if her were less. He hated this. He hated that he could let go of this resentment.

He needed to concentrate on the meaning of the broken fence. He had found out that none of the cattle or horses were missing, so he decided it was probably an accident by a traveler who had not chosen to disclose his mistake. But he had to be concerned that it might be more. He doubted there was an ominous meaning to it, since he had lost no property. But it was his duty to assure that no poachers, or cattle rustlers encroached his land.

He reached for the absent comfort of Melinda and instead pulled her pillow next him. A soft breeze came in through the open window chilling the room. Luke got out of the soft bed and padded across the cold wooden floor to the open pane. As he was about to pull it closed, he heard it again.

"Luke." The voice was clear and sultry against the coldness. "Luke, Come to me."

The seductive sound pierced him. "Hello? Who's there?" He spoke to the outside, where the voice came from. No one answered. Cicadas sang their noisy song. But no other sound replied.

There was a sharp rap at the door, followed by Caleb's concerned voice. "Mr. Logan, are you Okay?"

"Yes, I'm fine, just closing the window. Caleb what are you doing here?"

"Mama asked me to sleep in the spare room, Sir. She's still real worried for you. Says you haven't been yourself."

Luke slammed the window closed and yelled through the door with fury that surprised him. "Caleb! Go home now! This is my house! I decide who sleeps here! You're Mama has no right to decide what I can and can't do and where or when I do it!"

"Yes Sir." said the quivery boy in the hall.

Luke regretted yelling immediately. "Caleb, go back to the spare room, it's alright. I didn't mean to yell. Sleep at home from now on unless I invite you." He tried to sound calming as he walked to the bedroom door. He opened it and listened as the Caleb walked back to the room.

"Yes Sir, Sorry."

"Goodnight Caleb"

# 8

Luke walked into the kitchen where Melba was making pancakes and bacon. Luke ignored the hot food, found the bread and cut a slice, then went to the icebox for the milk. "Good morning Melba." He said.

"Good morning Luke." She replied coolly

"Melba, I am going to talk to the men and make sure no head are missing, I'm going to check on the horses and then I'm going for a walk. I am going alone. Do not send Caleb to follow me. I know you care, but I run this ranch. I own this house. I am tired of being disrespected. I am more than capable of walking without help." He finished the milk. Took the bread and turned sharply out of the kitchen before Melba could respond. He didn't even know if she had formed the words for an answer. He imagined she stood behind shaking her head at him.

He left the house and walked to the cattle yard. Charlie was there, along with a few men. They talked for a while and Charlie assured him no cattle we missing. "Nothing but a couple of chickens are missing, we're thinking maybe a bobcat. We all have to keep our eyes open."

"Thanks Charlie." Luke walked away thinking about the missing chickens and the broken fence. He checked on the horses, and considered bringing Bessie with him, but he felt like he could navigate better alone. He wanted to go back to the fence and see if he could figure out the problem. He knew nothing there would help but he felt like going anyway.

As he neared the area he heard men talking with gruff slurred voices. "Looks like they fixed the fence."

"Why ain't we waitin' til night time like last time?"

"We're not goin' in. I haven't seen Larry since he took off from us the other night and I wanna see if I can track him."

"Track him?! What are you an Indian?"

Larry's is my brother in law, Hattie is worried about him and if he don't come back... well I dunno and she's already wondering where I got the chicken and wanting more."

They suddenly became quiet and Luke realized they must have spotted him. He walked over to the group of what he guessed was about four or five with all the authority he could muster. He took his hand of the rail and hoped he didn't look blind. His hips felt empty as he missed the gun belt he hadn't worn for three years. "This is my property. You need to leave now, I'll call the sheriff and have you arrested, or you can leave and I'll pretend I gave you my chickens as a gift!"

"Sorry Mister! "Said a snivelly voice.

"Hey, Matt, don't you see he's blind? I think that's that Logan guy. Owns the place. He's worth big bucks. Take him we can maybe get a ransom or kill him, we'll figure it out later."

Luke froze for a moment, then turned and ran in the opposite direction of the voices. They had clambered over the fence and were after him. Luke's foot caught a rock and he was flying through the air. He landed on the hard ground with a thud. His ribs landed on yet another rock and his foot flared pain. He scrambled to get up. The men were close behind him. Before he made it onto his feet, large rough hands grabbed his shoulders. Out of nowhere a fist hit him hard in the face and he was nowhere too.

# 9

Luke woke up with a headache and throbbing pain in his left foot. He was lying on some blankets on a cold wooden floor. Cigar smoke, whiskey and body odor scented the air. The sounds were of snoring, and even breathing, the sounds of men very deeply asleep. He assumed that they had drunk themselves to a stupor and he felt pretty sure they'd be hard to awaken. He lay as still as possible and listened for anyone that sounded awake. Surely they had a look out. There was nothing to indicate a person was awake among the slumbering sloths. He could count three different men by the breathing and snoring. He felt his throbbing face it was puffy and painful and his right eye was swollen shut. He assessed the rest of himself and discovered his ribs were very sore to the touch and even a deep breath hurt. He supposed he had broken one or two; His left foot though hurting and swollen didn't seem broken. After he was certain that he was the only person awake, he got to his knees. He felt the area around him and crawled through the unknown room past the beds to his right. He crawled slowly and quietly searching in front of him for the door and hoping it was set opposite the window as he would expect it to be. The journey of what couldn't have been farther than fifteen feet seemed to take an eternity. His hand reached a wall. He chose to move to the left along the wall and finally found the door. He rested his hand against it and listened for what might be on the other side. Silence greeted him. He stood up slowly and tested his foot which could just scarcely bear his weight. He found the knob and turned it gradually so as to not make a sound and pulled the door open just as deliberately. He hoped no light flooded the room. He stepped out, waiting for someone to shout at him to stop, but no one did.

He was in a larger room and limped through it holding his left hand over his fragile ribs and using his right arm to search for hidden obstacles. His legs found a wooden box and he nearly tripped. The sound was thunderous and he stood as still as possible. The snoring continued uninterrupted. He made his way around the box trying to find the way to an exit. His route brought him to a wall and he felt along until he reached a corner and then a stove. Past the stove he at long last reached a door, it was cool under his touch and the sounds emitting from the other side were the sounds of the night. He opened it and stepped out into the vast unknown space.

He tried to get a feel of where he might be. There was nothing that he could sense. It seemed like probably flat rocky land, an old farm probably

The men had come from the south to The Double Jay, so Luke figured he should head north. Problem was, he had no idea which way was north. Luke decided that people commonly put doors facing the south in a home and so he walked to the back of the house and walked away that way. He really had no idea if this was a good choice but he had to make some choice. So he walked.

He hope he walked in a straight line, the ground changed from hard and rocky to soft and back again. It was tough going. He limped along trying not to feel the pain of his foot. He fell countless times. He had passed no buildings that he knew of. The ground changed once again becoming less rocky and grassier. He tripped over something jutting from the earth and found it to be a tree root. He was entering a forest. He searched his mind now for where he could be. There was a large woody area to the southwest of The Double Jay and he thought it could be that but there was a lot of forest area around. Entering the forest could be deadly. He knew it teemed with wildlife, and he would become more lost.

# 10

He chose a direction and walked along the edge of the tree line. He tripped and stumbled and his foot grew more painful. It was time to sit down and wait. He had limped for hours and had to be far from the farm house by now. He found a large old tree and sat at the base of it. He was tired and now that he sat the many pains in his body screamed out for attention. He couldn't do anything for the pains so he ignored them. He longed to take off his boot but didn't dare; he knew He'd never be able to put it back on again.

Luke knew his men would be searching for him so he stayed under his tree for now. He fell asleep and dreamed of Melinda.

*Luke was in a forest. Huge trees loomed around him. He could see a pathway and a light up ahead. Melinda was calling him. Her voice was desperate with fear. Luke searched for her as he ran through the trees, but he couldn't find her. He jumped over fallen logs. He ran and ran past the diverse foliage around him until he didn't think he could run anymore. He was exhausted. It hurt to breathe. He had to find her.*

*She cried out his name over and over "Luke! Please Luke! I need you!" Now her voice was right next to him but although he could see everything around him he couldn't see his beautiful wife. He searched with his hands out in front of him to try and take hold of her but his hands passed through empty air.*

*Now her voice was far away "Luke! Luke Come to me!" He tried to run toward her but chains bound him to a tree. He struggled against the heavy iron. His vision went dark.*

He woke up stiff and uncomfortable with the sun obviously well up in the sky. He was hot and moist with sweat.

"Luke!" it was her voice, pure and electric coming from very close by. A twig broke just feet in front of him and she was there, the owner of the mysterious and beautiful voice.

"Who are you?" Luke asked. He was anxious without cause. He half expected no answer again. She had proved herself a phantom and although he was sure she was there, she could be gone instantly.

"Luke, come with me."

"Who are you?! Why do you bother me?"

She gave a sultry laugh. "I bother you? No, you long for me. You desire to know me, and I desire to know you. I want you to come with me."

He was not used to people ignoring his requests and once again he asked her "Who are you? What do you want with me?"

"You intrigue me, I've been watching you."

"You've been watching me? How? What do you mean? WHO ARE YOU?"

"I am Celeste. I am not like anything you have ever known and I want you to be with me. I do not have to ask you. I can take you by force. I am giving you a choice. But I intend to get what I want."

There was a slender cool soft hand taking his hand and helping him stand. He sensed no effort in the assistance yet he was fairly pulled off the ground.

"Come." She said

Luke tried to walk but his foot would no longer bear his weight. "I want to go home. Can you please help me get there? I own the Double Jay Ranch."

"I know you do" she said in her silky voice.

Then quite unexpectedly he was being carried. Her arms were long and slender she was very slim. He could feel the bones of her shoulders and back just below her smooth skin. She seemed so small yet she carried him as if her were a baby. He strained to get down but her grip was tight and he couldn't move.

She walked so smoothly and quickly it felt like flight. Mere minutes later, she placed him on his familiar bed. Her arms held him in an embrace and she kissed his mouth with firmness and he felt himself surrender to an unspoken authority. She moved her lips to kiss him on the neck and he gave her sanction to be there and anywhere else she chose to go. There was an instant of pain, so quick so sharp if wasn't certain of its reality then exquisite bliss. Luke's mind exploded in pleasure and she kissed his neck and in a minute it was over. She laid him gently on the pillow, and said to him with her honeyed voice "I will be back to give you your choice."

Luke wanted to ask what she was talking about. He wanted her to continue that strange kiss, yet she was gone. Her absence was as obvious as her presence had been. He discovered he was too weak to move, or speak. He could only sink deep into his pillows and revel in the comfort.

# 11

Luke wasn't sure how much time passed or if he had fallen asleep, but he became aware of the door opening slowly. Then he heard Melba release a huge sigh. "Oh Luke! You're here! We've been searching everywhere for you! When did you get here? What happened? Oh my goodness you're hurt! Let me help you." She was next to him in an instant and when her hand touched his sore and swollen face she drew it back quickly. "Oh my lord! You are burning up with fever!"

Luke tried to answer her but he was too frail to speak, much less think coherently. He let her fuss over him and was grateful for it. She took off his boots and the pain in his foot shot through his body. Melba was frantic with worry as she undressed him washed him and redressed him. He let her do it all, though he really had no choice in the matter.

He was pretty sure he had fallen asleep this time but now he woke to find the doctor entering his room with Melba beside him.

Melba spoke gently to Luke. "Dr. Cullen is here Luke."

Dr. Cullen came to the bed and started touching prodding and examining immediately as he spoke. "Luke, I'm gonna check you out now. What happened?"

Luke finally found some strength to answer but could muster only an abbreviated tale. "Thieves at the south fence grabbed me…" He wanted to say more but truly didn't have it in him to tell the whole tale. He was faint. He was shamed.

Dr. Cullen uttered words here and there, and went over every inch of Luke's person. By the time he finished He had pronounced Luke to have several broken ribs, and a badly sprained left foot. He couldn't determine why Luke had a fever but prescribed penicillin for it. He wrapped Luke's ribs tightly, and ordered bed rest.

Luke laughed ruefully to himself. As if he could do anything other than lay in this bed now anyway.

## 12

Poor Caleb was assigned duty to take care of Luke's needs, while Melba came in several times a day to make sure Luke ate and drank and relieved Caleb to take care of his own nourishment.

Melba spooned broth into Luke's mouth. She spoke to him in the gentle voice one reserved for the very young or the feeble. "Good boy, keep it up. You're doing fine."

The hot savory liquid had felt very good going down his throat and didn't feel heavy in his stomach as it had that morning. Luke felt helpless. It was something he hated. Laying there in his bed being fed broth, he thought back to the war seeing his brother John in the hospital tent as an old woman tried to get him to take some water. John had been unable to swallow it. Luke had felt powerless watching his brother die in front of him.

Melba wiped Luke's sore mouth clean with a napkin, rearranged his pillows and laid him down. He listened to her gather the bowl, spoon and whatever other dishes she had onto her tray and exit the room. He enjoyed privacy for only a few minutes before Caleb came in and took a seat in the chair by the side of the bed.

"Do you need anything Mr. Logan?" He asked cautiously

"Leave me alone." He answered and tried to go to sleep. But nature called and though Luke tried to ignore it the urgency grew. He tested himself but couldn't even sit up without help. "I need the chamber pot." He growled.

Caleb quickly grabbed the pot and placed it under Luke's bed clothes. Luke suffered the humiliation with indignation burning though his insides.

Slowly Luke was regaining some strength but the fever wouldn't break. He sometimes awoke to cold cloths on his head, other times to cold cloths surrounding his naked body. He fell in and out of consciousness often. His dreams were bizarre and vivid.

*Huge hands held Luke down on the ground. They pressed his chest. They gripped him with fierceness that cracked his bones. Fists pummeled him from nowhere and everywhere. Melinda's voice called out in desperation. Luke struggled against the pain to reach her. Her tears poured from the sky like hot rain. He fought back at the fists. He tore through the countless hands holding him down but always there were more coming at him. Melinda began to scream his name begging him for help, and then she was abruptly silent. Then there was Celeste with her mellifluous voice calling his name softly. He could feel her manifestation next to him. Fists stopped their rampage. Hands loosed their grip. Her lips were on him gentle at first then more and more firm. With each second of her cold lips on his hot skin his power increased, the world about him came into view, blurry gray, then color, then sharper until he saw the tiniest details. He stood under a regal tree among many trees. He could see into the crevices of the bark. The veins that ran through each of the thousands of leaves contrasted the flesh of each leaf. Ants scurried in a tight formation up the tree. He watched it all in awe, trying to take in every minute detail. But Celeste took his face in her hands and made him look at her. He couldn't see her. She was a void. He wanted to look away and see the forest again, but she held him with that preternatural strength and kissed him again. His world was instantly gone, his strength vanished.*

Luke woke with a start. Caleb was there. "Are you Okay? Mr. Logan you're Okay. You're in your bed, at home. You're Okay." Caleb lightly touched Luke's hot and bony shoulder in an attempt to reassure him, he was safe.

Luke lay back against the pillows breathing heavily. He tried to keep his tenuous hold on the vision. But the dream was a mist now. Hot tears leaked down to intermingle with his clammy face and were wiped away by a cool clean cloth in Caleb's loyal hand.

## 13

Melba entered the bedroom with a bowl of wonderful smelling food. The scent of a rich beefy broth, herbs and fresh bread wafted toward him.

"Good evening Luke. I have dinner here for you." She sat the tray down and she helped Luke sit up in the bed. Then, once situated she began to spoon the broth into his mouth.

Luke closed his mouth and turned away in the perfect imitation of a grouchy toddler. "Let me feed myself Melba. I am not a baby." He was so tired of being ill. He was sure he could do something as simple as feed himself.

"Mr. Logan you're still so weak... I just didn't think you were ready yet."

"Give me the bowl." He snarled.

She put the bowl in his hand. It was heavier than he thought it ought to be. He could barely hold it. He found the spoon and shakily moved it toward his mouth spilling it before it reached its goal. The hot soup burned his skin and burned his spirit. He tried to throw the bowl across the room but his frailty allowed him to drop it roughly to the floor instead.

"Luke! Oh you spilled the soup. Let me go get some more!" Melba cried.

"I'm not hungry. Just get out!"

Melba did not get out although Luke's rage filled the space. She hummed quietly as she deliberately cleaned the mess. She didn't care for his refusals as she changed his bed clothes and linens. She never said a word, just hummed soft familiar tune. Then when he was securely tucked in to a clean bed, leaning against fresh pillows, she put a glass of water in one hand and two small pills in the other. "Take your medicine, drink that water. Get some sleep you'll feel better tomorrow." Then she left.

He did as she said.

## 14

He woke up. It was the middle of the night. Caleb was in a bed down the hall and Luke could hear the light sounds of the regular breathing of his sleep. Crickets chirped outside.

Celeste was there. He knew her presence. Her scent was musky and ancient with a hint of lilac.

"Celeste, how-"

Her finger lay gently on his mouth. She spoke with sensuality. "Come with me forever. I offer you more than you can fathom. I offer you strength, power, me. I offer you life eternal. I can give you unimaginable abilities. I can give you sight."

Luke's mind raced with questions. Her last statement had stopped them all cold. "Sight? I could see? How? What are you? Why do you want me?"

"I am not human. I am something more. I am all powerful, I will live forever and I can give you that gift, for a small price. I am intrigued by you. I can make men do whatever I desire, but I can't compel you, because you can't look into my eyes. I am fascinated by the strength of your spirit. I am enthralled by you. No one has ever held this power over me. I want to give you my power. I do not want to be alone anymore. I want someone by my side, someone like you." As she spoke her siren's song, her words attempted to captivate him the way her eyes normally would.

"What's the price?" he asked, interested but not yet captured. "And you could make me see?" Hope caused him to believe her somehow.

Before she answered she took him in her arms again and kissed his neck as she had before. He felt the thrill of ecstasy for a few seconds and then she laid him down again.

"You would just have to give me some blood, accept some of mine, as an oath of devotion to me. It's easy to give me your devotion. I'm beautiful. This life of power is well worth it. You give up infirmity and gain immortality; you give up dependence and gain superiority. My blood heals. My blood comes with eternity."

That voice, that scent. Celeste dripped allure. Luke tried to sit up but couldn't do it. Her kiss had weakened him. She lifted him easily to a more comfortable position and arranged the pillows behind him.

"Come to me."

The bedroom door opened and with a tiny swish of air she was gone, and Caleb came in.

"Start knocking! Allow me some pride!"

"I'm sorry, I heard you talking and thought you might be having a nightmare again or maybe were in pain. Do you need anything?"

"Bring me some water and some pain medicine." Luke said gruffly

The boy grabbed a glass and the vial of pills and gave Luke what he asked for. "I sure hope you feel better soon Mr. Logan." He said, his feelings hurt, Caleb returned to the room down the hall.

Luke lay back against his pillows. Caleb was a good boy. Luke regretted being so harsh. He just hated being so weak. His mind went over everything Celeste had said. Her voice caressed his mind. What was she? Who was she? She was not human that was clear, but he couldn't wrap his mind around the possibility that there were some who may appear human and not be. She had invited him to become what she was. Celeste was certainly unearthly. She was more ethereal and yet more real than anything he had ever encountered.

His mind grew fuzzy as his pain decreased and he fell asleep.

Luke woke up to knocking at the door. "Come in!" he said weakly.

"Luke, I'm going to rewrap your ribs and check on how you're doing." Said Dr. Cullen. The thin middle aged man came to Luke's bedside and immediately began his poking and prodding accompanied by utterances that only he knew the meaning of. When he finished he sat back leaving Luke more sore than he had been before. He handed Luke a pill and without much thought Luke swallowed it. "Well, you still have that fever. I can see you're bruises and everything else healing just fine. Your ribs have a few weeks to go. I'm going to give Melba a recipe for willow bark tea and you will drink that twice a day. I'm also ordering an ice bath and Caleb is going to keep cold cloths on you until it breaks. It's not going to be comfortable young man, but we have to break that fever."

Harvey carried Luke to the bath and laid him gently in it. Then ice began to pile up on top of him. "Watch his ribs!" shouted Harvey to some unknown person who didn't answer. Soon he was shivering in the tub of large chunks of ice. He at least had been allowed the decorum of his night shirt but having the ranch hands see him so helpless burned Luke worse than the fever. The cold was more uncomfortable than he could imagine. He couldn't move out from it. He struggled against the weight of the ice and labored against the enclosing cold. The cold seeped into him and he shivered so violently that he felt as if his ribs were cracking all over again. He finally let the dark void of unconsciousness take him.

Caleb was faithful to the doctor's orders. Every couple of hours he was in the room wrapping cold wet sheets around Luke. He had lost his timidity and ignored Luke's struggles and rebuffs as pathetic as they were. But Caleb spoke to Luke with kindness, care and love. Caleb remembered the kind strong man when he wasn't ill. He knew this angry hurting man was not the real Luke Logan.

Every time Luke began to hope that he would feel better, warmer or more comfortable. Caleb showed up, removed the drying sheets and replaced them with god awful freezing wet ones wrapped tightly around Luke's spindly body. At last evening came and the wet sheets were replaced with a warm and cozy set. Luke felt flimsy and tired. He let Melba feed him a rich broth, he swallowed the pills she gave him and he melted into the bed to sleep.

# 15

Musky ancient lilacs filled the room and brought Luke to awareness. "Give me your answer." Celeste spoke into his ear.

"Yes, heal me. Yes, I'll be what you are. Yes, I will be powerful." He said it urgently so she couldn't leave again.

"It's nearly dawn; I want to finish this before anyone wakes up. Celeste cradled Luke in her arms and kissed him on his face, then on his chest and then his neck. There was a momentary sharp pain gone quicker than he could register it, and then he felt the warm rush of joy. Heated ecstatic elation filled him and flowed from him Rapture exploded in his mind. Then she laid him softly on his pillows. He was in a weak stupor.

"Now tell me," she said. "Tell me you are my loyal servant. Tell me you will give me all I ask. Tell me I am your master."

He could feel Death's icy grip. This moment he could breathe one last time or he could say yes with that same breath. "Yes" it was barely a whisper, all he could manage to push out of him.

Celeste lifted his hand and placed it on her wrist. "Take this" she said and moved it to his mouth. His trance didn't allow him shock at the blood dripping from her open wrist into his mouth. The taste of it filled it and the ecstasy was back but to a fuller degree. Pleasure grew moment by moment as the blood went down his throat. He pulled it from her hungrily sucking life and strength into his being.

She pulled away from him. "Good, it is done." I will return to see you later, someone's coming."

Melba was walking toward the door, her familiar footfall apparent even from the bottom of the stairs. He could hear her soft words as she spoke to God, asking Him to heal Luke. He could smell her distinct odor, and more. Everything in the house had made itself known to him, Caleb in the water closet down the hall, a mouse hiding in the kitchen, porridge on the stove. All of these things were crystal clear but there was no vision, not a single color, shadow or shape was there. He could see the same abyss as always. But his new vitality overcame his disappointment. He jumped from the bed and opened the door before Melba could reach it. He rushed down the stairs and took the woman in his arms. "Your prayers are answered Sweet Melba! I'm healed!"

He felt the rush of her heart and the explosion of shock and joy at his sudden appearance. "Oh praise God! Oh Luke we need to get you back upstairs! Oh my! Oh my!" She cried.

He kept her in his arms as he led the way up the stairs and he smelled the overwhelmingly beautiful smell of the blood pumping through her veins. He was starving for it. But the irreconcilable desire was suppressed and instead he kissed her wet cheek.

## 16

Celeste arrived in the afternoon. Luke introduced her to all those present. He didn't bother with a story on who she was or how he had met her. He had been catching up on ranch business with Ike and Harvey when she arrived. Melba was in the kitchen fixing a huge celebratory meal for the entire ranch. Food was how she celebrated everything.

Caleb sat in the room trying to make himself invisible so no one would throw him out. He was thrilled to have Mr. Logan back. He seemed healthier than ever now. Caleb was proud that his hard work caring for his friend had paid off. He had never seen a woman that looked like Celeste. She was small and slim with a tiny waist Her blond hair was done up in a complicated knot on her head. Her skin was pale almost see though. She wore and expensive looking frilly dress unlike anything Caleb had seen in Willow Lake.

Although Luke couldn't clearly hear the thoughts of the people around him, he could sense their mood, and a sort of topic of mind. Some like Caleb had more open minds and he could almost get a monologue of thoughts. He laughed to himself that Caleb thought it had been his ministrations that saved him. He also loved the boy's loyalty and kinship. He needed to make sure he rewarded him somehow. He was certainly not going to kick him out of the room.

"Celeste and I need privacy to speak. We are going for a walk." Luke faced Caleb "Caleb, I appreciate your protection, but I don't want you to follow us. Do you understand? I need to be completely alone with Celeste right now."

Caleb's surprise registered through his whole body. "Yes sir." Luke had known he was in the room?

Celeste spoke up then in her unidentifiable accent. "Luke, I have brought my carriage. We are going for a ride. I'll have him back before the dinner." She addressed the latter to Melba who had just come into the room.

Melba thought the woman rude haughty and cold. Where had Luke met such a girl as that? He'd best be home for dinner. This ranch was long overdue for a celebration. Her Luke was finally well again. She wasn't going to let one snotty girl ruin the party.

# 17

    Celeste and Luke walked arm in arm out the front door they appeared to be lovers to anyone who looked out. Luke felt no love toward her right now. He had pledged devotion and he knew it was more than a pledge. He knew he was compelled to do her bidding. He was angry though. He had not expected this power to come with this dark desire for blood. Who in their right mind fed on blood?

    Celeste led Luke to the carriage and he found his footing and climbed aboard. Celeste stepped up in to the driver's seat and they took off.

    "You told me I would be able to see! I can't."

    She answered nonchalantly. "Well I thought you would be able to. But you're alive, and you are powerful certainly you can feel the difference."

    "Yes, I can, and it's amazing, but... I am hungry. No amount of food is satisfying me. I want blood! I nearly killed Melba this morning. Ike cut himself shaving and when he walked in the room I wanted him so badly, I had to leave. I couldn't even tell them why I was leaving because there were fangs in my mouth where my teeth should be!"

    "I suppose I should have mentioned the blood to you before. Oh well. Let's go get revenge Darling, then you will not be hungry anymore." She said flippantly.

Luke seethed, but the mysterious promise of gratification and the newness of the world around him allowed the anger to turn to excitement. He could hear all manner of birds, animals. The warmth of the sun touched his skin and air was filled with a myriad of scents. Flowers, and trees and dirt, and homes all around him intermingled to create a picture of sorts. Each scent and sound belonged to itself distinctly. He knew there was flowering bush with tiny animal curled up below its shade, just as well as he knew that Celeste was wearing Lilac scented lotion.

The carriage stopped and Luke got a sense of where they were. They were in a pasture one hundred feet away from a large amount of rotting wood. He could smell a fire, and coffee and some sort of cooking meat. It was a cabin. He knew it was the cabin he had been taken to by the thieves. As they got closer he counted five people inside he heard them arguing and knew one was a woman.

Celeste didn't bother knocking at the door. She opened it and walked in as if she owned the place. Luke stood by her side. "Sit down. Do it now and do it quickly."

Everyone but Hattie complied. She backed up to the wall in the kitchen area, breathing heavily filled with terror.

"Woman, look at me, sit down. You have nothing to fear."

Hattie sat down and the panic left her and the men, they were empty and stunned, awaiting further direction.

"Luke come here, let me show you." She took his hand and placed it on a man's head. "Push his head back and you reveal a very beautiful large vein in his neck. This is an easy place to choose."

Luke could smell the blood, his desire was immense. He hated this man, he wanted this man to suffer for what he had done to him. This disgusting thief couldn't be called a man. Fangs grew from Luke's mouth and he lunged to the throbbing vein. Blood flooded his mouth and filled him with pleasure. He drank deeply as the thief's life poured into him. He tasted the man's life. He knew the man as he drank the blood. This was Ephraim, husband to Hattie, hungry, desperate and mean. This was the only son of poor parents. This was a man that fought in the war and come home to find his wife mourning the loss of their children and nearly starving, herself. This had been Ephraim and now he was no more.

Luke dropped the dead man on the floor. He was no longer hungry. The taste of Ephraim's blood was fresh in his mouth and the taste of Ephraim's life was fresh in his mind.

Celeste had killed Hattie and one other man while Luke had drunk Ephraim. Two more sat terrified in wooden chairs compelled against everything to move.

Luke leaped for one of them and punched him hard in the face. "Here's some of what you gave me!" Luke hit him repeatedly. The man's pain burst through his mind. This man had made Luke feel helpless. He had nearly killed him. Luke hadn't been able to fight back. Now his rage exploded and Luke pummeled the man with abandon. As Luke hit him the man's pride crumbled to shame and Luke laughed but continued hitting until he was hitting a lifeless body.

"What a waste of food," Said Celeste as she finished off the last man. "But I don't want to be a glutton. You're covered in blood from beating him. Come wash off."

While Luke washed off by the pump, Celeste broke several bottles of whiskey around the cabin. She grabbed Luke, lit the cabin on fire and flew toward the carriage.

# 18

In the carriage on the ride home Celeste used the time to teach Luke. He wanted to talk about what had just happened but she ignored his questions "We are, what is called by some, vampires. We can live forever. The only things that can kill you are fire, beheading and a stake through the heart. I don't know what you know of vampires, but much of the lore is wrong. Obviously sunlight can't hurt us. We are not afraid of Christ. We don't believe what He has said. God is a liar. If you don't have blood, several liters, about what you'd find in a man, about once a week you will weaken. The more blood you take the stronger you will be. You can eat food but it will do nothing for you, except to help keep your secret. You must keep this a secret. We are not the only ones of our kind. Our survival depends on our secrecy. If you tell anyone, other vampires will immediately know and they will kill you and the poor soul you told. We have many powers, not all of us have all the same powers but the common powers are strength, invulnerability, the ability to move very fast. Most vampires have a deep and powerful sight." She laughed. "I guess you won't have that. Vampires are able to compel, we can hypnotize, but this involves the eyes, I don't think you can do it. I know I couldn't do it to you. I would have taken you against your will long ago. I guess that's one more reason you will have to stay with me. I don't know how you'll manage to kill effectively without compulsion."

Luke mulled over what she said and what he had done. He had enjoyed taking the lives of those men. He had enjoyed getting his vengeance. But he also felt evil. Was he evil now? Did he have to kill? He had wanted vengeance only once before and that had been for Melinda. But when he witnessed the hanging that exacted that revenge the sounds of death had given him only the briefest satisfaction. When he swore his allegiance to Celeste, had he given up any goodness inside him? He wanted to ask Celeste, but he felt that would be a very bad idea.

She had said she wanted someone to stand beside her, but it was clear to Luke she wanted to lord over him. She made sure he knew she was in control.

Celeste was haughty she was completely without concern for anyone other than herself. She could charm people with her looks (Caleb told Luke how beautiful she was) her voice and a pretense of personality, but she lacked any deeper virtue. She loved the fact that despite his inability to disobey her, he needed her beyond that since his blindness took away his ability to induce compliance from others. She held this fact over him. But Luke sensed there was more to this life than she let on. He believed she could be teaching him more but she liked his dependence. She especially loved to put him in a position in which he required help. He had never been degraded like this before, even by the now dead thieves.

# 19

Once a week they went out together for what the ranch hands thought was a walk or ride, but was actually a hunting trip. They always went at night. Often they would walk to the large forest and once hidden from view, Celeste would take Luke in her arms and fly to some far off town or city to hunt. Celeste chose the victims. Luke had no choice in it. The vulnerability of these people was in direct proportion to the evil he felt.

One night, while the people at the ranch believed them to be walking in town, Celeste took Luke to a large city, further away than he had ever been in his life. She preferred Cities as people didn't so easily notice a death. This one was crowded and dirty. The ambience was sullen. She never bothered to tell him where they were, unless she thought it might benefit her. They walked together up the crowded cobbled street past a busy bar. Outside the bar was a woman, she smelled of old sweat, cigars, perfume, and disease. Celeste walked up to her and said "Take us to your room Darling."

The girl, Luke realized she was much younger than he thought, started to protest with revulsion at taking a man and woman up to her room. Celeste touched her roughly and got her full attention. "Take us up, you don't mind. We're going to have fun and you are going to make a lot of money."

Immediately the girl was excited about the money and looking forward to something fun.

They went through a nearby door, and up narrow stairs in a small building with people populating many of the rooms. They entered a room, and Celeste wasted no time. "Go get a friend to join us, you'll both have so much money you won't have to work for a week."

The girl left to fetch her lucky friend. She could barely be sixteen years old. Prostitutes were a favorite of Celeste. Only the boss noticed they were missing and if he cared too much he made for a feast.

"Celeste, she's a child!" Luke argued.

"Hmm, I was her age once, no one cared that I was a child. She's nothing. And I'm sure, even you can tell she's dying. We're doing her a favor ending it now instead of letting her go slowly. Consumption is a terrible way to die."

The girl entered the room with a friend in tow. The second was barely older than the first and just as small. She had just put on some cheap perfume to try and mask her body odor. Luke and Celeste would not be her first customers that evening, but they would be her last.

# 20

Luke took his usual walk to check on the ranch. He stopped to speak with Harvey, with Charlie and the others to make sure everything was running smoothly. Then he continued along. He considered inviting Caleb to walk beside him instead of trailing behind, but he wasn't in a mood for conversation. He had a lot on his mind. He had become a monster. He was evil incarnate. There had to be some way to make up for the malevolent creature he had become. He wanted to stop killing but he craved the blood, and if he didn't kill the others, he was in danger of killing the members of his staff, his family. He needed the blood by the time the weekly hunting trips came about. He could hear blood pumping through his friends. He smelled its delicious odor. He could think of nothing else by the day of the trip. His longing for the blood nearly overpowered him. The bliss that rushed him took over him. The lives that came through that blood filled him.

But even so he had tried once to not kill a man that Celeste had told him to kill. The man had been a simple beggar on the street of one of Celeste's cities. He had had no debauchery in him. He was only hungry and poor and too feeble-minded to gain respect or employment. Luke had told her no.

"I said this is your dinner, and it will be. Drink!" She spoke with a coldness that could only come from a frozen heart.

Luke's feet moved against his will. Tears poured from his eyes. He reached for the man, who Celeste had not bothered to calm with hypnotism. "I'm so sorry." He bit into the man's throat and drank his life away. Despite his hate for the deed, the blood did its job on him. His mind burst with pleasure. He laid Tom Wilson gently on the ground, stood and faced his maker.

"You have blood all over your face fool. Wipe it off." She said frigidly. "You are too sentimental. Don't you understand these are below you, especially an idiot like that man? Be careful about your silly sentimentality. I thought you were a man. When you cry, your tears are blood. You've given up your soul, you've given up true tears. You're worse than girl!"

Luke used his handkerchief to wipe his face clean. Celeste grabbed his arm and dragged him toward her. She wiped his face hard to let him know he had done an inadequate job. Then she walked away, leaving him in the alley with Tom.

He knew that she hoped he would grope after her or be lost. He followed her regardless of her efforts to shame him. But he was careful not to catch up too quickly. Her rage could turn violent quickly. He had no problem navigating people and hoped no object on the road below would impede him. She moved fast until she reached the outskirts of the city and he reached her minutes afterward. She took him without speaking and they flew back to the ranch and walked hand in hand to the house in the ruse of loving couple.

Celeste usually came to the ranch two or three times a week to keep up pretenses of a romance. She stayed away for nine days after that event. By that ninth day Luke feigned illness and ordered everyone to stay out of his room. The longing for blood was an unbearable lust. He had also begun to feel weaker.

When Celeste arrived, he played the happy lover and whisked her out of the house before she could finish greeting people. He apologized for his insubordination and promised to never again resist her. Then they went hunting and he impressed Celeste by taking two people that night.

Luke had come to realize that Celeste did not possess his ability to gauge feelings. That was his special power. He found that when he had recently fed he could more easily read the thoughts of others and as time passed the ability grew. He could not read Celeste at all. He had a notion that all vampires would be beyond this ability.

He had tried to fly the way Celeste did, but he couldn't. She had bragged to him that flying was a rare and powerful gift. He had not shared his ability with her and he planned to keep it private. Keeping a secret from the cruel woman made him feel as if he had some power over her. He tested himself regularly to see what other skills he possessed. He had found the strength and speed she said were common. His amazing sense of smell and hearing were also common. So far only he had not discovered another power. But he felt Celeste was being secretive, trying to hold control over him. She was hateful, vindictive and cruel. She enjoyed watching her victims suffer. Luke couldn't imagine spending an eternity with such a monster but he saw no way out of the situation.

# 21

Luke prepared the bank draft with Ike's guidance, and handed it to his foreman. "Ike, take this to Fellowship Church for me this afternoon. From now on, I want money to be donated to the church every month."

"Fine, Luke. It's an awful lot of money, especially since you don't go to the services. You know Melba would love to have you come with her and the family."

"I know Ike. She has been inviting me since I was a kid. I want to donate to Chief Running Bear too, will he accept money?" Luke asked

Ike had grown up with the Shoshone Tribe who had been forced to live on land twenty-five miles south of the ranch years before. "Sure he will. Luke, why are you giving all this money away all of a sudden? We have here money for the church, my family, the orphanage in Willow Lake and trusts for Melba's boys. What's going on with you?"

"Nothing, I've been fortunate, I'm just trying to do some good." Luke answered. He had to find a way to do some good. His soul felt vile. He'd hoped that this would make it feel better, but the screams of prostitutes, beggars and thieves rang in his ears.

Celeste and Luke sat alone in the parlor. Melba had lit a fire in the fireplace. Celeste sat on the opposite side of the room and Luke sat next to her. No one was around but they spoke with the quiet voices of secret holders.

"Tell me why you speak of Christ and God as if they're real. Why do you say God hates us and that He's a liar?" Luke was curious about Celeste's favorite topic. She could rant for ages about God.

"He is real. I've spoken to some who saw the propaganda of Jesus of Nazareth themselves. He and his Father rejected us. He promises his followers eternal life, but he doesn't deliver. He calls them to an imaginary heaven. He enslaves them on earth. My father and my mother were devout followers, but they died, when I was six years old. They had told me every day, if I followed Jesus, I would live forever, I would go to Heaven, and I would be happy. Then they were killed, and I was left alone. I wandered the streets a beggar until I grew into enough of a woman to work on the streets. I sold myself just to eat. God didn't take care of me. I thought he wasn't real by then. But then I met Zacharias, he turned me and taught me. He showed me God was real by showing me those God kicked out of Heaven were real. What kind of god has no mercy on even angels? How could he throw them away from his protection? How could he not care? Why does he lie to people, dupe them into lifelong service only to let them rot in the ground?" Her voice had become louder and more passionate as she spoke.

"Caleb is coming." Said Luke. We have to stop this conversation. Here drink some of the coffee Melba made for us."

Celeste changed immediately from cold hard monster to charming sweetheart. Luke knew that most of the people on the ranch knew she wasn't sincere. They didn't like her and some thought she was after Luke's money. But he never told her. He liked this little bit of power over her. He knew things she didn't. He knew she wasn't as effective as she believed herself to be.

She had never told him anything about her past. Zacharias was her maker. How old was he? Who could she have met that had actually seen Jesus? Could that vampire still be alive? She had met demons? Demons were real? He wasn't sure what he believed. But he knew she believed that God was real.

He longed to be apart from Celeste at the same time as he desired to be with her. She must have something to teach him. And he couldn't understand if it was the blood they shared or just her but he loved her the same way he loved the blood. She filled his mind. When she came near him, his heart skipped a beat in hope. But that hope was always dashed. Her voice was the same as the call of the blood. This strange love, made him accept her abuse.

He wondered if he should try hunting without her but didn't know if he could. He hated the killing and loved the blood. He hated being a murderer but the blood sent him to the heights of ecstasy. Even when he wasn't hungry he longed for the high of the blood.

# 22

Celeste had refused her invitation to the ranch Christmas party. The staff was all relieved to not have to deal with the woman on such a festive occasion. A huge decorated tree stood in the corner, with gifts piled high underneath. Valerie, Charlie's wife played tunes on the piano with Hank accompanying on the guitar. Melba supervised the extra help hired for the occasion as they passed out cups of hot cider, hot chocolate, and a plethora of pastries and other treats among the guests. A long table was loaded with a variety of foods. All the staff and their families attended as well as the children of the Willow Lake Orphanage and the couple who ran it. Very few of the ranch hands had families, most were single men but a few lived in town and came to the ranch daily to work.

Luke had made sure to get a gift for each child in attendance. He had the tree decorated with oranges and apples. He encouraged the children to take them off the tree as they pleased. Joy and warmth filled the large ranch house, reminding him of his youth with mother, father and brother gathered for holiday parties. He sat in a far corner unobtrusively observing the merriments.

Harvey passed gifts out to the children, calling each name as he pulled the package from beneath the tree.

"Amy! I have a box for you. I wonder what's in it." Harvey said

A diminutive girl filled with wonder that there was a gift for her stepped forward to receive it.

"What do you say?" reminded Mrs. Peterson, the orphanage 'mother'.

"Thank you." Squeaked the tiny awe-struck voice.

And so went the process until every child present had received a toy. Luke also had bought each orphan a pair of shoes and a coat but he had those delivered to the orphanage as a new bounty of gifts for the following day. Most had never received a Christmas present before much less two or three at one holiday. Even the children of his staff would be fortunate to receive more than one gift.

Luke enjoyed the feelings of appreciation and delight the children were experiencing. He sat back and fed on the happiness of the parents as well. So much joy gathered together in place nourished his dark soul. He actually felt content right now.

Melba tried to coerce him out of his corner seat. "Please, Luke you need to socialize, tell everyone hello."

He used an old excuse. "So many people, Melba, it makes it hard for me. I'm enjoying the party form here."

"Okay." She answered, knowing his stubborn streak wasn't going to give in. So because he wouldn't go to the others she sent people to him to say hellos.

He felt like a king or other noble accepting tribute, although he accepted only their greetings, thanks and conversation.

Before the orphans left the party they gathered together and sang with sweet high voices songs about infant Jesus come to earth. Then they came one by one to Luke and said "Thank Mr. Locan" and left board the wagons that would take them back to Willow Lake.

# 23

Luke gained the reputation of philanthropist over the next several years. He gave money to every charity he found worthy. He gave time and help to most who asked. The people of Willow Lake and even the surrounding towns thought Luke was a wonderful and generous man. Luke didn't see himself the same way. He saw a black hearted monster.

Caleb was now attending university to become a doctor, and Luke paid the way. Luke admired the young man's good and open heart. It seemed in direct contrast to his own evil one.

Celeste and Luke walked the dark streets of a distant city, satisfied after their gory meal. Celeste had important things to discuss with Luke. "You'll need to make some changes soon. You will always appear to be twenty three years old. Soon enough someone will wonder how you look so young. You're going to have to leave your ranch. It will continue to make money for you, while you and I travel. I think we should go to Paris. It's a huge dirty depraved place. No one would notice us."

"I don't want to leave my home."

"Too bad, you'll have to. You can stay away for twenty or thirty years, come back to an entire new staff, as your son. I have a lawyer that will handle all your finances. He'll make sure that as you grow older through the ages, your fortune will grow and go with you. He'll send you a new identity every few decades. You have no choice. You will go. We leave in six months. The lawyer will contact you soon."

Luke was crestfallen. He mourned his home and the people that had become family to him. He saw the wisdom of her plan.

At dinner the next evening, Celeste shocked everyone including Luke by announcing their wedding. She also announced to everyone that she and Luke would be leaving the ranch and travelling for an undetermined amount of time. Luke was furious with her for going behind his back and telling people in such a sudden manner. He had not thought marriage would be part of the plan. He'd wanted to break the news of his departure gently and privately. He could feel the dismay of everyone in the room. They were let down. Ike wondered why Luke hadn't told him already. Melba was forlorn at the thought of losing him and wondered how Luke could not see what a cold woman she was. Harvey was concerned for Luke's safety, and all of them were angry that Celeste was stealing him away.

Luke assured everyone that they would still have jobs no matter how long he stayed away. He put Ike in charge of the ranch in his place, and put Harvey into the foreman position. He didn't care at all about Celeste's wedding plans. She knew it and didn't care. She kept him informed of everything. She went over Melba's head and hired a cook to make an elaborate meal. She travelled with Ike to the nearby Shoshone and asked the holy man to perform the ceremony, further upsetting Melba by not having a church wedding. Ike did it for Luke's sake.

Luke was glad that they would keep it limited to ranch staff and families. He was repulsed by the idea of a wedding and marriage with Celeste. She assured him that it would not be a legal marriage. But the people at the ranch needed to think it was.

"Why do we have to pretend we're married at all?"

"This gives you reason to go abroad. Everyone knows you'd never consider it unless I made you, plus it will explain the existence of a son when you return eventually. Do not question my plans.

## 24

Luke walked through the fancy Parisian apartment. He was bored. There was no work to do, and no one to talk to. He had once longed for solitude, now he longed for companionship. He didn't enjoy much of what the city offered as entertainment. Operas, Symphonies, and the like were not his style. He found the formal clothes all those activities required cumbersome. He hated the stiffness of the gatherings he and Celeste attended.

City life held nothing of interest for Luke, except for the surprise of ease in navigating alone. He walked the city streets, exploring for hours at a time. Ike had given him a walking stick and showed him how his grandfather had used a staff to walk alone with ease. Luke grabbed the cane and walked down to the street. Between the cane and the minds of people around him, he walked swiftly and without difficulty.

He couldn't remember why he had chosen this life. There was nothing to enjoy about the power and "gifts" Celeste had offered. Weren't gifts supposed to be free? He had paid too dear a price. Had he wanted his sight so badly? His empathy was almost like having sight. His supernatural strength, speed and fortitude made life nice. And when people thought he was weak, he knew his strength even if they didn't. but he still wasn't happy. Killing made him sick to his stomach. His desire for the blood was revolting, and worse than all else the joy the blood gave him disgusted him.

Celeste didn't live in the huge apartment. She kept her residence secret from him. She showed up when she chose to show up, which was rarely more often than once a week. She would arrive in the apartment and tell Luke that they were going to an opera or a society party and expect him to be ready in an hour.

## 25

He strode past the townhouses and apartment buildings along the fancy street. Smells of coffee, and baking bread mixed with flowers, and sewage. Women strolled along wearing expensive perfume. Men smoked cigars. The moods were often nonchalant, or bored. But he found other moods as well. When he found a mind that piqued his interest he would listen in, explore it and often follow it.

A woman sat in a café. She was desperately sad. Luke sat down at a table not far from her and delved deeper into her mind. Disconnected thoughts floated toward him. The name Andre was there. He had cheated on the girl with Michelle. He was leaving her. As time passed, Luke's telepathy and empathy both matured and he could read thoughts now just as easily as emotions.

The girl finished her coffee and walked away. He followed from a distance. She hadn't noticed she had a follower yet. She was incredibly melancholy. As she walked her depression deepened. Andre and Michelle danced through her mind. She imagined them together. She imagined them laughing behind her back. She didn't want to go home. Everything there reminded her of Andre. She turned on to a side street. She must have past the apothecary shop. She stopped in front of it and her thoughts turned to poisons.

Luke grew concerned for her. She continued walking and Luke eased a little. But he became alarmed when the girl remembered a bridge spanning the river a few blocks away. He felt the plan cement in her mind. Her step quickened. Her mood almost brightened.

He didn't know what to do. He walked closer to her. She now registered his presence with a little alarm and some disappointment that perhaps she wouldn't be dying today. Luke was relieved but knew it wasn't enough to truly stop her if she were serious. He followed her to the bridge careful not to scare her. She realized he was blind, and disregarded him. His own annoyance at her disregard welled up. He almost decided to show her how dangerous he truly was, but self-restraint let her continue to think he was a harmless nothing.

She stood at the railing of the bridge looking out at the water but not seeing it. Her thoughts were of Andre and their affair. She relived all the hurts. She stepped up to the rail and prepared herself to climb up. She saw herself a martyr. She imagined Andre's reaction to knowing it was his thoughtlessness that caused her death. She gained bravery from knowing how this would hurt him.

"Excuse me Miss," Luke said, trying to sound destitute or at least lost. "I was wondering if you could tell me where is the Rue du Beouf? He had learned French quickly probably due to his ever strengthening mind power and spoke it beautifully.

She was stunned by the question and paused, looking him over before answering. He listened to her opinions as she decided he was harmless and she would have to help him. She stepped down toward him. "Yes, it's just that way." She answered, probably pointing.

"I'm sorry, Miss could you perhaps take me there? I'm blind." He answered.

"Oh, certainly."

He took her arm and let her lead him to the street he requested. "Thank you, I had an argument with my friend and stupidly I left him. Now I realize I don't know where I am. I hope your father will not be angry with me for allowing you to accompany me alone. I have no ill intention. May I ask you, why are you unaccompanied, Miss?"

"I am an independent woman Sir. I can go out alone if I please!"

He was glad to feel her anger rising and her depression dissapating. "I apologize I meant no offense. I'm in debt to you. My name is Mr. Luke Logan." He bowed slightly.

"Mr. Logan, I'm Noelle Bellanger. Are you American? You speak French very well."

"Yes, I'm American. I have decided to sojourn in Paris. Miss Belanger, I would love to thank you for your kindness, perhaps before we reach La Rue, I could thank you by buying you a cup of coffee and a pastry?"

"That's quite improper Mr. Logan, but I am an improper woman. I would love to." She answered. He could feel her intrigue. The impetuous woman had lost her desperate desire to die completely, now she was all rebellion and dare. She already had formed the plan to hurt Andre and upset her father by dating an American, a blind one at that.

They stopped at a small café where Noelle ordered a coffee and a croissant. Luke ordered a coffee and drew his mind back so he could enjoy her company. She was a stubborn young woman who enjoyed upsetting the establishment. Luke had no issue in letting her use him. He found her amusing.

Luke did not disclose his new friendship to Celeste. She didn't mention it, so Luke guessed she didn't know. She only came to him when it suited her. She was busy with other things. He wondered what took her time but was happy to not deal with her. She must have tired of him. What if she grew so bored of him she stopped coming to him at all?

# 26

Luke had a new plan on his daily walks. Instead of easing his boredom by following some emotion that caught his attention, he now searched the minds around him for the void that would signal another creature like himself. Maybe another vampire would answer his questions.

Luke needed to find out if there was more than Celeste was telling him, and what it was. If he could have a secret friendship with a human, perhaps he could find a vampire. He had to find out if he could leave Celeste. He had to find out if there was another way to exist.

Months passed before Luke found what he was looking for. But he wasn't on a walk. He was with Celeste at an Opera. He sensed a space where a mind should be. He knew there was a vampire among the crowd. He wondered if Celeste knew. The vampire moved over to the pair.

"Celeste, it's a pleasure to see you this evening." He spoke English with an accent Luke couldn't place in a deep gravelly voice.

"Sabatok, How are you? I'd like you to meet my companion Luke Logan." She said.

Luke presented his hand and it was clasped by a strong large hand with smooth skin. The grip was sure and radiated kindness. It seemed completely foreign to imagine a kind vampire. Of course he had only ever met Celeste. She was as cruel as anyone he could imagine.

"Do you have plans after the opera?" He asked "I would love for you to join me at a party being thrown by Monsieur Christian Gladue. He is the benefactor of the opera. There will be rich blood gathered." He added the last with a hint of humor.

Luke was thrilled at the idea of spending time with the enthralling man. Celeste snuffed the idea. "No, Thank you Sabatok, we can't"

Luke was courageous in the presence of someone else. "Celeste, dear, I would love to get to know Sabatok and I think we can put off our plans for a couple of hours."

Celeste fairly growled and he knew there would be consequences when they were alone. "Well then, thank you. We'll be happy to join you."

They left to find their seats. Celeste gripped Luke's arms so tightly he felt the bone crack beneath the skin. The pain was horrendous and although it healed in less than ten minutes the agony of the healing was just as bad as the original break. He acted as if nothing was happening. He grit his teeth. His face was cold with sweat. But he wouldn't give her the satisfaction of a reaction.

She seethed in silence as she dragged him by his broken arm to their private balcony. When they finally reached their seats she spoke with icy calculation. "Do not undermine me again, or you will be sorry."

Luke remained silent and didn't speak again until they were among the company of the other party-goers. He and Celeste acted the role of happy couple with Celeste holding him closely to her side. They met the cream of society. They raved about the new soprano and spoke about the upcoming opera season. Luke didn't care about any of that but pretended he did.

Sabatok came to the twosome and took Luke's arm himself. "Mr. Logan, I'd love for you to meet some friends." He was gone with Luke before Celeste could protest. Luke guessed he would have more broken bones later and decided the price was worth the opportunity.

"Sabatok, I hope to get the chance to speak with you alone sometime. There is so much I would love to ask."

"Celeste is a cruel woman and not quite sane, Mr. Logan You need to be free of her."

"I swore an oath, she's my maker and I've no idea how to go on without her." Luke spoke in whispered conspiracy.

"I understand, and I will help you." The brave vampire answered quietly, then followed in louder in French with: "Mr. Logan I would like to present Miss Elaine Mangin, the soprano and diva of the opera."

"I'm so pleased to meet you" said Luke as he started to search for her waiting hand. Sabatok placed Luke's hand under the sopranos, and Luke bent to kiss it.

"Charmed" spoke the bored but bell-like voice. She must have greeted dozens in just this manner. Luke wasn't even sure she looked at anyone she met.

Sabatok and Luke moved on. Sabatok once again spoke English in hushed tones. "I say this now only because I believe Celeste is otherwise engaged presently and is not listening, but you and I will speak further. I swear I will not forget you."

They arrived back to Celeste to find her embracing a man. Luke smelled the blood immediately and his lust peaked. She was feeding in the middle of the party! How dare she? She finished and put the man down in a chair. He smelled of brandy. Luke supposed the dead man appeared drunk. He was very angry, and he was very hungry.

"Ah, Luke, come, I would like to go home. Thank you, Sabatok for the invitation. I enjoyed myself thoroughly. I'm sure you will be headed home to Egypt soon and we won't have another chance to see you." With that she walked out of the party.

Luke followed her through the crowd as best as he could. The people that noticed him stepped out of his way with slight revulsion for the pathetic man. He caught up to her as the carriage and driver arrived. She boarded it without Luke and left.

She was punishing him. She was so childish, and selfish. Luke asked the servant at the front steps to hail him a carriage gave the driver his address and went home.

# 27

His hunger roared at him. He wanted blood. He left his apartment and walked along the streets. At this time of night this neighborhood was quiet, but a few streets away he knew that degenerates reveled. He reached the street he sought, and inebriated fuzzy minds met his. A prostitute offered herself to him for a price. The smell of her blood overwhelmed everything else about her.

"Take me to your room." He said

She walked down the street into a little alley and into a compact doorway. He followed her down the hall and through another door. She sat down on the bed "Come." She said.

Luke searched her mind. This was Marie, she was hard and worn. She had very little emotion about her. Luke went to her, pushed her head back and started toward her neck. He was about to kill someone of his own choosing. Somehow the conviction not to kill by choice was stronger than the desperate desire for the fluid pumping through her. He stopped, pulled bills from his wallet and tossed them at her. He turned and left, and when he exited the broken down little building he moved at preternatural speed to his home.

He was evil, yes. He had killed countless people, and had enjoyed the results of the killing, but he had never killed without Celeste's orders. He always had made her tell him to do it. It was a silly little nuance, a thin line. But it was a line he wasn't prepared to cross.

Luke knew she was furious and wanted to teach him a lesson it could be a very long time before she came back to hunt. He was pretty sure he would have to cross that line soon, but not tonight. He could stand the hunger. It had only been piqued by Celeste's feeding on the drunkard at the party. Hunger would make him stronger, he was sure.

Luke met Noelle the next day for a tour of an art museum. She found it delightful to see the paintings and sculptures. She described them in great detail showing off her education to him. He had expected to be bored but she truly enjoyed the art and therefore he enjoyed it. He had thought there had been a bit of malice in her invitation. Why else would she have invited a blind man to look at art? Walking with her and listening to her describe what she saw proved to him he was wrong.

"I hope you're not bored. I wasn't thinking about your blindness when I invited you, I was so excited for the new exhibit and I enjoy your company" There was no lie in her words.

"You are delightful company Miss Bellanger, and I am appreciating your vivid descriptions. You must really love art."

"Oh, yes, I do. To take something that was simply clay or rock or canvas and transform it with hands, chisel, or paint into something better, fascinates me. I studied art at the college, I was the only woman in my class." She trailed off leaving something unsaid. Luke allowed her, her privacy and didn't enter her mind to guess what it was.

A few minutes later she perked with an idea. "I have a friend, a wonderful sculptor who creates beautiful pieces. We could go to his studio. He would let you see his art for yourself. You could touch anything he made. I know he would let you."

Luke liked the idea. "Yes, wonderful, can you arrange for us to go tomorrow?"

"I'm sure I can." She said. Meet me at our café at two. It's only a short walk from there.

## 28

Luke arrived home to find Sabatok sitting at his piano playing an exotic tune. "Hello. I didn't expect to find you in my home but I'm really glad you're here."

"Now begins your education. You are new. Yes? Maybe five years old?"

"Celeste turned me six years ago. You are the only other vampire I have ever met."

"I will not be the last. Some are dangerous like Celeste. Some are not. She's older than many you will meet and sometimes as a vampire gets too old she becomes unstable. She forgets her human self, or she feels all powerful and entitled, or like Celeste it's all of this and more."

"Who are you Sabatok? How do you know Celeste?"

"I am ancient, much older than most vampires I've ever met. I first met that v al creature when she was young about three hundred years ago. She was cruel even then. I think she's lived a very hard life both human and fiend. She is not my concern at present. You are hungry, why haven't you fed?"

Luke didn't know how honest to be with Sabatok. If he told him about his disgust with killing would the seemingly sympathetic vampire think he was weak? But if he told him that he had never hunted w thout Celeste then he would seem even more so. He chose to trust. "I abhor killing. I have only ever done it aga rst my will. I'm very hungry but I can't bring myself to kill."

"You don't have to kill your prey. There are many ways to take a drink and eave your victim none the wiser."

Luke was astonished and hopeful. "Please Sabatok, teach me. Take me under your wing, if we can keep this secret from Celeste and teach me. She's withheld a lot from me, I'm certain of it."

"Of course, right now you're too hungry, you should never wait this long, try very hard to not get this hungry, it makes losing control a large possibility. You must always keep in control of your desires if don't want to inflict harm. Follow me. I knew you seemed decent. I hate for you to be stuck with her. I have not killed a human in a thousand years. You must maintain control of your nature if you want to feed without killing."

The two left the lavish rooms and strolled to the darker side of town. "The first and easiest way to sneak your taste is during an intimate moment. As you kiss her you take a nip and a sip." He laughed a deep and gravelly laugh which was surprising coming from the elegant man. "I just made up that little phrase myself. I quite like it. 'nip and sip' Ha."

They entered a large establishment that really reminded Luke of the saloons back home. Someone played a piano, drinks poured freely and conversations were loud. "The girls here will kiss you and beg for intimacy just to get a few coins from your purse. You won't even have to hypnotize them."

"I lack that particular ability." Luke said ruefully

"Ah, I wondered," Said Sabatok, "no mind, I rarely use it myself."

The two men took a seat at a table and moments later a young woman arrived, she reeked of cheap perfume, and liquor with a touch of mother's milk. Luke wondered how old the child was and why she wasn't home caring for it. Where was the father? He entered her mind but found the child was nowhere in her thoughts she was thinking these men looked rich and she needed to stroke their egos.

"Well, hello sirs. What can I get for you two very handsome men?" Shall I bring a bottle of whiskey or perhaps some cognac." She was already stroking Luke's shoulders. Instinctively he took her hand to his lips and kissed it, then moved to her wrists.

"Now" came Sabatok's voice so quietly only a vampire could have heard it.

Luke bit into her wrist and continued his 'kiss' Her blood filled his mouth and the ecstasy filled his mind but then her wrist was pulled roughly away. "Just a little. A kiss now to heal the wound. Remember you are taking just a sip there will be others." Luke kissed the broken skin on her wrist. He'd had no idea his kiss could heal anything.

"Thank you dear, bring us a bottle of your best cognac." Said his mentor to the departing girl. "I understand your hunger but you must use restraint." He said it with compassion, not the degrading that Celeste used.

"I didn't know I could heal the wounds I made." Luke said

"Yes, your saliva, your spit, your kiss, whatever you call it, will heal the wound after you bite, and numb the skin as well. The girl has no idea you took blood. I do think she might be a bit dizzy though since you drank just a little more than you should."

Sabatok and Luke danced with several women and Luke gave each his dangerous kiss. The restraint required to keep it small was huge. He settled for tiny explosions of bliss rather than body racking rapture.

The vampires left and walked back to Luke's apartment. "You must be a charmer, a seducer of women. Live as if you are young and free and take your sips often. Do not go more than a day if you can help it. I'll return. I know you have much to learn." And he was gone that quickly.

Luke was furious that Celeste had never told him such simple things like he had just learned. To know he didn't have to kill was wonderful.

## 29

That afternoon He and Noelle met and walked a few blocks to her friend's apartment and art studio. Luke was expecting a Parisian, but instead Noelle introduced Luke to a young American named Paul Mathews. Paul was the youngest son of a wealthy family had had been sent to study art in Paris and now chose to live here and work on his craft. He was wiry and passionate with a slight air of conceit. But after even a short visit Luke could see he had a compassionate heart.

He was very excited to show Luke his work, and led him gently from piece to piece. He would let Luke run his hands over the stone and would await his thoughts, then would give Luke his own description and thoughts on the piece.

Luke ran his hands along the cool stone and found a mustang reveal itself to him. He could feel her muscles and the wind whip through her mane. She ran without constraint. "She's a wild mustang. She's running free and fast. Nothing can stop her. She is joy in stone. She's beautiful!"

"Right, exactly! I really wanted to let her freedom shine through. She's black onyx. As you can tell she's running." Paul was as excited as Luke and quite proud to have his work so appreciated.

Paul led him to another figure, this one was not as hard a stone as the previous. Luke ran his hands gently over the carving of a tree and found a girl curled up asleep at the base.

Each sculpture was different and wonderful. Each revealed the beauty of this man's heart. Luke wondered what his life blood would taste and feel like.

After looking at all the pieces, Luke requested to buy the onyx mustang and offered Paul an exorbitant amount of money for the sculpture.

"Thank you for your kindness Mr. Mathews" said Noelle in a coquettish voice as they prepared to leave.

"Yes, thank you for allowing me to see your work. Please keep me informed of any new pieces, I enjoyed this experience so much. Your talent is very evident."

The young American was nearly giddy over the whole experience himself and walked Noelle and Luke to the building's exit. "I certainly will, Thank you Mr. Logan"

Luke could easily have carried the statue back to his home, but since it weighed in excess of fifty kilograms, doing so would have questioned his humanity. He had it delivered and placed near the window of his luxurious apartment. He often ran his hands over the cool stone, seeing the horse, and imagining her joy.

## 30

Two weeks passed before Celeste showed up in his rooms. She expected to find her fledgling weak and desperate. She was incensed to discover him vital and content. She needed Luke to need her. She ignored his vigor and instead said "That ugly stone thing doesn't match the décor at all."

"I like it and I could care less if it looks good to you. It's beautiful to me." He spoke with a confidence she didn't like at all.

"We're going hunting. Did you get so desperate you turned to vermin?"

"Vermin? No" He could feed on animals? He filed the fact away "I have hunted just fine without you Celeste. I don't want to go out this evening."

"You think you don't need me? You were lucky. You would die without me, either at the hand of an enemy, and there are many out there that would murder you, or because of your feebleness."

"I don't need you Celeste. I'm fine. I think it's you who need me." He was tired of her and angry.

Celeste's rage was barely held in check. "I need NO ONE! I am superior to any I have ever met. You are an idiot. I'll release you to your ridiculous notions. Soon you'll beg for my protection. There are many vampires out there who will kill you for the strength they would gain. Or you'll get caught fumbling around for your food and some brave foolish human will kill you. I do not need anyone especially a sightless weakling like you. I chose you. You could have been great. Now you'll be dead."

Luke laughed at her fury knowing it would enrage her more. "I'm just fine."

"I should kill you myself!" and with that her wrath let go on Luke. She gripped his arm and flung him across the room to hit the wall. He may as well have been a rag doll. Before he could react, she had him and once again threw him. He hit the ceiling and landed on the ornate table. She held him down with one arm and scratched his face deep and hard repeatedly until his visage was shredded. She kicked him. He felt every rib break. His lungs were punctured and both arms and legs were cracked in multiple places. He lay unable to move under the great pain as his body slowly healed itself. She screamed with fury and without word, as she continued to pummel him.

There was a great sucking of air and she quite suddenly stopped the beating and became silent.

Sabatok spoke with deadly deliberation "Get out now Celeste, if I ever see you again, I will kill you. I will kill you the way I killed your maker."

"I won't come near you or Luke again! She was cowering.

Luke had no idea that she was so afraid of Sabatok. Her terror was as obvious to Luke as if she had been human.

"Swear it!

"I swear it. Please, let me go, you'll never see me again." She was gone and Luke thought Sabatok had thrown her out the open window rather than allowed her to fly away.

"Drink." He said in his deep timbre but now without anger only sympathy.

Sabatok's open wrist was at Luke's mouth and the blood entered. Luke would have enjoyed the high but the blood was busy healing his many broken bones and organs and the intense pain rebounded through his head. Soon Luke was being cradled in the large vampire's arms and carried to his bed.

"Why was Celeste so afraid of you?" Luke was shocked at how weak he was as the blood healed him.

"I killed her maker, she has made oaths to me. She knows how powerful I am. Sleep now" Sabatok said and Luke obeyed.

# 31

When Luke woke up the next day, he was not only completely healed but much stronger than he had been before and elated that he was free of Celeste. Sabatok's ancient blood had enhanced Luke. He felt the power running through him. He reached out his mind and touched the beings in the vicinity. There was a couple making love in an apartment below his. A man contemplating a marriage proposal walked past the building. A hungry child begged for bread in a nearby doorway. All these and more came to Luke with just his slightest effort.

He dressed quickly and ignored the mess of the previous night. He grabbed a satchel, and his cane and went to find the beggar. In the street he found young Gerard hungry and needy. He didn't approach the child.

He sat down at a café and ordered a large breakfast of breads and cakes. The boy saw him and noted his rich clothing. He longed for just some of the food on the rich man's table.

Although Luke felt incredibly powerful, he made every effort to appear harmless. He made a show of his blindness in order to give the impression of mildness.

The timid boy came near him and said, "Excuse me Sir, do you have just a little money. My mother and I haven't eaten in days."

Luke handed the boy a sweet roll. "I thought I was hungry, but I'm not. Will you please take this food for me?" he put the breads into the satchel and inconspicuously added a roll of money.

"Thank you!" Said the truly grateful awe-struck Gerard

"Go straight home to your mother now."

The boy ran off toward his home, stuffing the roll into his mouth and thinking about the feast he and his mother would be enjoying in a few minutes.

# 32

Sabatok and Luke sat on the summit of a frozen mountain in some Asian country. The old vampire was teaching his student. He loved to take him to exotic and secluded places for their lessons. Neither vampire was bothered by the effects of the freezing bitter fast blowing wind.

"One thing I ask you to never do is to condemn another soul to our vile life. It is not a thing to be done easily or lightly, but I beg you to refrain from this act. It may become tempting over the years when you wish for a companion whom you do not have to withhold secrets. But, please be strong, give in to my desires, and do not do it."

"I won't do it Sabatok."

"Be careful not to make an oath to me. A vampire's oath to another vampire is a sacred unbreakable thing. Breaking it will have dire circumstances."

"Like what?"

"If you break an oath to another vampire, he has the right and the very strong desire to kill you. He'll be called across the earth to find you and murder you. And you will be as vulnerable to him as a human."

"So if Celeste came near me again…"

"I would know it, I would find her and I would kill her. She would be as weak as an infant to me. I would break her in half. Oaths should never be taken lightly, regardless of who is involved. Words are powerful. Some words carry incredible power. But let me continue our original lesson. I have learned something curious over the years."

"As you know I existed before Christ came to earth. Where I was born we knew of the Hebrews and their God, but we had our own myriad of gods to worship. I was a high priest to a King and I led him in worship of many gods. So I was aware of Christianity as it spread after Jesus, and I was aware of the powerful God they served, but I didn't care. I actually saw Him speak once. It was a huge crowd. He spoke of such things. He was enthralling. I don't know why though. Except for his words He seemed so ordinary. Of course now we know He was not ordinary at all."

"But the followers of Jesus, they can't be turned. I saw this when a vampire I knew tried to take one for his slave. He couldn't turn him. He wasn't even able to compel him to do certain things. I was fascinated so I tried myself. I chose a man who had been imprisoned and was about to die for speaking about Jesus. I took him, and did all that turning requires. But the man woke up a man. I tried to compel him to drink my blood and he refused. I let him escape from the prison and I watched an entire guard of Roman soldiers killed for his escape."

"Some of those that call themselves Christian, can be turned, the very religious ones among them. But there are some, the few I believe to be the true followers of this Jesus. They have something, some sort of seal or protection that keeps them safe from us."

Luke contemplated this. He had never thought much of Christianity one way or another. Melba had been a devout Christian. She had always been singing or humming a hymn. She had brought her boys to church every Sunday. She had spoken to Luke throughout his years about Jesus. But he'd never listened. Now he contemplated this might be more than some religion, there might be more to it. But it didn't really matter. He knew he was beyond any redemption for his evil deeds. He knew it doubly now, for if a Christian couldn't be corrupted then he couldn't be made pure.

Luke had more questions "The vampire lore is much more myth than reality. Humans think we can be harmed or killed by the sun, a crucifix, garlic, and holy water. They believe us to be in a state of death during the day. Why?"

Sabatok answered thoughtfully, "People believe what they need to believe. Those few that suspect vampires exist, give us weaknesses and restrictions to feel safer, some were created by vampires themselves so that people would believe we are more vulnerable than we actually are."

## 33

Unlike Luke Sabatok was a social creature. He loved gatherings. He and Luke were at a different party almost every night of the week. Operas, Symphonies, and their after parties, weddings, birthday celebrations, and a multitude of other festive occasions made up their schedule. He allowed Luke to beg off a couple of times a week for his own pursuits. He understood Luke preferred a more quiet life. He even sympathized with the solace Luke found in solitude. But in order to live without killing Luke had to learn to be more social.

Most people believed them to be Uncle and Nephew, although the men looked nothing alike. Sabatok's ancient Egyptian genes and Luke's blonde hair and blue eyes didn't lend itself to the belief that they were related but people just accepted this as a fact. Luke often called Sabatok 'Uncle' when they were at parties. He couldn't know how different they really looked from one another but he paid attention to people's impressions of them. He knew Sabatok was an unusually large muscular man with dark olive skin and deep set black eyes. His nose was long and straight with something that reminded people of a hawk.

People saw Luke's blonde hair and blue eyes shrunk smaller form lack of use in a wide set. He had tanned skin from long hours walking outside. His hair was thick and hung to his shoulders. His shoulders were broad and his waist was slim. He knew people found him very attractive. He had felt women's reaction to seeing him.

Luke thought Sabatok must push people to believe their kinship. Sabatok told him that people believed what they chose to believe. They think what is easiest and safest. "You'll find friends who won't notice that you look the same as you did five years before, even ten. They just accept your youth and forget you should age with them. I wouldn't give it longer than ten though for our secrets sake. But people dupe themselves all the time so they won't have to see the reality around them."

# 34

Luke and Sabatok were on a beach on a tiny island thousands of miles from anywhere Luke had known existed. Behind them was a jungle teeming with animals Luke couldn't picture. Sabatok taught Luke he could live off the blood of animals if he had to. "If you ever travel by ship, rats can sustain you. Anytime it's not prudent to take your little sips or if circumstances keep you from people, animals of any kind can be your dinner. But felines they hate you. They will scream at your presence. They will either try to get away from you as quickly as possible or they will try to rip you to shreds. So my advice is to stay away from them in general."

Luke and Sabatok walked along the dunes of a vast desert. "I don't think Celeste told you this but it's vital. You can never tell anyone that you are a vampire or in any other way tell them this secret. It is an oath you made to all vampires when you became one of us. If you ever break this oath, you will be killed. Whoever you told will be killed. Never reveal that you are a vampire. It's why I killed Zacharias, Celeste's maker. She had already, in a jealous fit, killed the poor girl who had learned the deadly secret."

Celeste had told him about keeping the secret but not about her maker's death. "There are so many oaths. I never thought they were so important when I was human."

"They are very important. Always be careful with your words. Words hold great power."

# 35

*Luke gave the skeletal woman a loaf of bread. "Do you think this changes anything? You've killed too many. You steal blood and enjoy power on the suffering of others!" she accused. He walked through the streets of London and everywhere bloodless corpses littered the path. They pointed at him, and blamed him for their condition. He threw money at them. But it didn't change anything "You did this! You!" Tears wet his face and rained on the bodies as he ran and ran trying to escape them. "Your bloody tears can't help us! Nothing can help us!" They moved crawling toward him arms outreached and seeking. No matter how fast he moved they kept up. Their cold dead hands gripped his feet and his legs, entangling him. He fell into the gruesome mob. They pulled him into their ranks.*

Luke awoke with a start. Dreams were a very rare occurrence. Over the last fifteen years of his travels around the world he'd dreamt only five or six times. Always the dreams had been similar to this one. He got out of bed and found the bowl and pitcher. He cleaned his face and smelled the blood wash off. He dressed in the stiff clothing of aristocracy and longed for his comfortable ranch clothes.

He had kept up with happenings at the ranch and had his lawyer send letters to them every few months in which he told them of an imaginary life. In which Celeste had given birth to a son, named after his father, and Luke and his happy family traveled the world together. He sent souvenirs to his ranch family at times as well.

He had been saddened to read about Harvey's death and eventually Melba, Ike and most of the men he remembered. Caleb had indeed become a doctor. His brothers Eli and Marcus now ran the ranch. They had stopped asking him to return home years ago.

# 36

Luke's favorite preoccupation was still walking. He had to think of what city He and Sabatok were in now. Sabatok rarely stayed anywhere longer than a month which gave Luke very little chance to get completely comfortable in his surroundings. They did revisit most places and had their favorite hotels. Luke stretched his mind and decided they were in Istanbul, one of Sabatok's favorite cities. Luke spoke the language reasonably well. He in fact learned languages very quickly and spoke them with ease. He decided this was some sort of extension of his empathic and telepathic abilities.

Sabatok was immensely more powerful than Celeste had ever been, but by his own telling he was thousands of years old. He told Luke very little of himself he had alluded to being a priest in Egypt during his human life. But his years made him extremely powerful. He could send fire out of his hands. (That was a truly impressive skill) He flew, but told Luke he had not always been able to fly at first. He had developed that skill after several hundred years. He could fly very far distances in very short time. He could move things without any physical touch. His original special gift had been his ease in compelling others. While most vampires had to make eye contact and speak directly what they wanted Sabatok had only to speak with intention and the victim would do everything he wanted, or even feel the way he wanted him to feel. It had developed now to the point that Sabatok didn't even have to speak. He just pushed his thoughts toward the person. He was very careful to use this power very sparingly. Luke noticed he used it most often to calm people and situations.

He had taught Luke a lot. He had introduced Luke to many others of his own kind. With Sabatok as his mentor Luke had an automatic protection from any vampire who might plan to harm him. He found that the majority of vampires chose to live either solitary or in a group of two or three.

Vampires respected one another and lived by unofficial rules that that respect warranted. But most of the vampires he had met thought of humans the way Luke thought of cattle. They lorded their superiority. Most chose not to live among humans. Most preferred the night, enjoying its darkness.

Luke enjoyed living among humans. He didn't feel superior. He wanted desperately to make up for his evil by doing as much good as possible. He didn't want to forget his humanity the way some vampires had. Sabatok too spent a good deal of time with humans and if it helped this ageless creature hold onto his humanity it could do the same for Luke.

Luke wanted to return home to The Double Jay Ranch, but Sabatok explained to him that he could never go back. "How can you pass for a son? You're blind. Why would your son be blind?"

Luke had looked forward to his eventual homecoming so much over the last twenty years it had never occurred to him that the plan was flawed. Of course! His stupid blindness had gotten in the way again. He rarely let it. More often he didn't even think about it anymore.

Sabatok was like a caring sweet father. "I'm sorry son. You can't go back there as long as anyone is alive to remember you." He gently kissed the bloody tears from Luke's face as a father would kiss his hurting child.

## 37

Luke was despondent. He ran his hands over the onyx mustang. He wanted to be home more than he wanted anything else. He'd left behind all the people he'd cared about. Now he knew he'd never see Caleb or Eli or Marcus, or any of the others again. They thought he'd chosen cold cruel Celeste over them. They thought he would rather travel the world than be at home on his ranch. He couldn't let the depression turn to tears. It became stone cold anger

He walked out into the Istanbul roads. He reached out his mind and found a man a few blocks away with obvious malice in his heart. He searched the man and listened to his evil plot. The man was holding a large sword turning it back and forth in his hand as he thought of his brother in law and business partner.

Luke moved quickly and stealthily to the home of the man. He stooped outside listening to the man's thought and feeling his hatred. The man stepped outside to fulfill his murderous plan. His rage blinded him to the well-dressed blonde man that stood in wait.

Luke reached out and grabbed him. He dragged him back into the little dwelling. The man's vile blood scent was ambrosia to Luke. With one swift and graceless stroke he ripped the man's throat out and drank deeply of the villainous life. There was no anger or depression any longer just pure blissful rhapsody. He dropped the cadaver. Luke stood reveling in the afterglow of the blood.

He took a deep breath and reality hit him. What had he just done? He had just killed with joyful abandonment. He hadn't even thought about it. He had murdered. He had enjoyed it. He was disgusted with himself. He scanned the area and found it thankfully empty of anyone nearby. He found the fire pit in the center of the room. He could find no liquor or wine, and wished for Sabatok's power. He found a large amount of fabric piled on a couch he covered the man's body with the textiles and lit it on fire. He hoped it would appear he had been murdered in a more natural manner.

He went back to his hotel room as quickly as he dared. He ran his hands over the onyx mustang and longed for a long fast ride on Bessie in the wide open fields of home. He thought it would be awesome to fly through the air, anything to try and outrun his malicious soul. Did he even have a soul? How could he murder so easily and take such pleasure in the act?

He swore to himself he would never again do something so abhorrent.


Luke and Sabatok sat over cups of steamy coffee in a crowded café. Luke faced his dearest friend in the world. He was full of shame. "I lost control Sabatok. I was upset. I don't remember choosing to kill him, but then he was dead. I'm so sorry."

Sabatok took Luke's hands into his. "Son, you don't have to apologize to me. You lost control. Don't bother with the guilt. Forgive yourself. Move on. "

"I can't just move on. I'm evil. I've proved that repeatedly. Now I've let you down as well."

"You're not evil. You have no choice about drinking blood. You lost control. I can't blame you for that. It happens. I am very old, and very strong, so of course I don't lose control but have been a vampire barely thirty years. It will happen. Forgive yourself. Keep trying to do what is right. I'm not disappointed that you gave in to your nature."

Luke was relieved that Sabatok didn't think less of him, but he couldn't help but think less of himself. Only an evil being would kill so easily.

# 38

Luke walked the streets of New York City. How long had it been since he'd been in America. He'd missed America more than he could have imagined. New York was nothing like Willow Lake Nevada but it was as close to home as he'd felt in more than twenty years. He entered the law offices of Constantine, Carey and LeRiche to discuss his business and finances. These were international lawyers specializing in the needs of vampires. They had offices worldwide but kept a low profile. Celeste had introduced him to the firm but he liked them. Sabatok spoke highly of the supernatural attorneys.

A human receptionist welcomed Luke to sit down and within a few minutes another woman appeared to lead him to the office of Mr. Wells. Luke sat down in a comfortable leather chair in an office that smelled of leather, books, and ink. They took care of Double Jay business and moved onto finances. The firm had done amazing things with Luke's money. He was rich beyond imagination. The Double Jay Ranch was now part of 'Logan Meats'. Luke increased his annual gift to the orphans. He set up trust funds for Caleb, Eli and Marcus' children. And now the hardest part was to come. He arranged for Mr. Wells to travel to Nevada and give them the notice of his passing as well as to read them his will and let them know that his son Luke Jr. would inherit the company and most of his fortune but the Ranch itself would pass onto Melba and Harvey's sons. Luke said a silent deep felt good-bye to his beloved home.

## 39

Victorian New York was as different from The Double Jay Ranch as anything could have been. He may as well have been in London or Paris except for the language. He wasn't willing to continue his endless travels. He planned to tell Sabatok this evening at the Art Gallery opening.

He missed Noelle's passionate and vivid descriptions of the artwork but he settled for a hired girl along with her thoughts and emotions. The artist sometimes would have compassion for him and allow him to touch the sculptures they created. He especially enjoyed that. Wealth, good looks and such an apparent vulnerability as blindness went a long way in procuring kindness from strangers.

Luke could barely remember what he looked like but he had heard himself described enough to know that most people found him handsome. He used people's thoughts about his good looks and even the pity some felt to advance his needs. He didn't care about pity. He knew who he was and had stopped caring what others thought of him long ago. Perhaps, he had reached that point because he was always aware of others thoughts. He usually found whatever pity or other negative thoughts vanished after he spent time with them.

Sabatok and Luke made their rounds of the art gallery separately and would meet to converse near the end. Each vampire took his nips and sips where he could. Luke flirted with Lily, the girl he hired to take on his tour of the gallery. She was young barely and adult and quite giggly. He thought these city girls were all much less mature than the country and town girls. By the same age a town girl was a woman. He had been barely older than Lily when he had been a husband and ran a ranch alone.

He put aside his annoyance with her and flirted away, as he took a little drink. He listened to her description in two ways, verbally and emotionally so he enjoyed the art. He and Sabatok approached some sculptures about the same time and greeted each other warmly, making unnecessary small talk for Lily's benefit. Had they enjoyed the paintings so far? Yes, Yes, what a promising artist.

"Lily, please request of the sculptor permission for me to touch his creations."

"Yes Mr. Logan, just wait here, please."

The artist agreed and accompanied the small group as they looked at his pieces.

Lily introduced him as Frances Butler. The artist was intrigued by the blind man's interest in art, especially his appreciation of paintings.

"Sir, how is it you enjoy paintings you can't see?"

Luke was impressed by his directness. "When it comes to the paintings it's the descriptions and reactions of the viewers that I enjoy. I do get a feel for the artist. I think my need for a description enhances the enjoyment of the describer as well."

They were at the first sculpture now. Francis surprised and annoyed Luke by suddenly taking his hand and placing it on the statue in front of him. He described the statue with the passionate pride Luke so liked about the artists he had met. Luke let the annoyance go. As Francis practically dragged him to the next piece, Luke pretended to trip. Francis caught him and Luke took a quick drink from the man as he struggled to keep him from falling. Francis never noticed.


After the gathering ended Sabatok and Luke took a carriage for a long ride back to the hotel. Luke took a deep breath and prepared to break the news to his friend and mentor. "Sabatok, you've meant the world to me, you rescued me from Celeste, you taught me how to make it in this dark other-world. I love your company. I love you the same way I loved Ike and nearly as much as my own father."

"But" interrupted Sabatok as he took Luke's hands within his own

"But," continued Luke. "I'm done travelling. I'm going to settle down somewhere, probably Chicago."

"Chicago, I've never been there, but I've heard it's a great town. I'll visit you often."

It was that easy. Luke hadn't known what to expect but he hadn't expected it to go so easily and quickly.

Sabatok even helped Luke to find a home. He had much more luxurious tastes than Luke. Together they chose a very nice place that Luke also found comfortable. He hired a young artist and paid him to choose furniture for his new home that would match his tastes. Luke was very happy with the results. He privately appreciated Sabatok's touches of opulence. It was a great relief to Luke to finally be somewhere he call his again.

# Part Two

# 1

Luke stood behind the counter of his soup kitchen passing out slices of bread to the unfortunates waiting patiently in the line. The current times had not hurt his wealth, but they had wounded, even destroyed too many. The crash on Wall Street, The droughts, and a general laziness had created a state of economic and emotional depression. Logan Meats opened soup kitchens in several major cities. They expanded their business interests to include wheat for flour, and corn as well, in an attempt to keep all their employees working.

Luke showed up at the soup kitchens to work on a nearly daily basis. No one knew he was the wealthy owner of the large company. They just knew he was a well to do kind young man who wanted to help the growing population of the poor.

Maggie stood by his side spooning soup into bowls. She was an art student at the college who believed she could change the world. She kept up with politics, and blamed the world's governments for the current situation. She was a buxom ginger spit-fire. Her parents waited patiently for her to tire of socialism and step into her role as socialite. Although disappointed by Luke's blindness they still held hope that Maggie would marry the quiet but rich young man. Maggie had no plans to marry at all. Had she been born thirty years earlier she would have been a suffragette. She would always find something to fight for and someone to protest. Luke knew that she would also find someone to love and marry, but it would probably not be someone her parents approved of.

He enjoyed her company and she enjoyed his. Both knew that this was a causal relationship not headed for marriage. One of the things that had attracted one to the other was the knowledge that neither wanted matrimony.

After the meal at the kitchen was done, the couple headed to the Clancy Street Children's Home, another organization owned by Luke. The children had no idea that it was their benefactor that visited them. They enjoyed the kind man, who told them vivid stories of the Old West, and made up colorful stories of adventures in faraway places.

They gathered around him as he walked in the door. "Mr. Luke! Look I made you a drawing!" came the squeaky voice of Peter, a small five year old.

"Thank you Peter. Where did you get paper? How kind of you to use it for me?"

"Mrs. Foster brought us a bundle of newspapers and Miss Maggie gave us coloring pencils. So I drew you a picture of Cowboy Hank. I like his stories best of all. Tommy drew you a picture of a pirate but mine is bester than his."

"I'll bet they're both very good Peter." Luke took the picture from the child and walked in a sea of tiny legs and hands to the sitting room and the chair that had become his 'story telling chair'. When he wasn't there it was Mrs. Fosters knitting chair.

Mrs. Foster entered the room and welcomed the young man. He came faithfully every Sunday afternoon and it was a highlight of the week for the children. It gave her a very thankful respite as well. But she spent it listening to his stories just as raptly as the children. He spoke of places as if he had been there.

More than just Peter and Tommy had used the precious paper as a gift for Luke and he accepted each one with gratitude. Some of the children understood he was blind, some didn't. They all knew he needed help sometimes to find things or that if you wanted to give him something, you couldn't just hold it out to him. He was a grown-up that didn't know they were raising their hands for permission to speak and they would have to say his name to get his acknowledgment. The older children knew he was blind. They had accepted him long ago.

"What kind of story do you want to hear today?"
"Cowboy Hank!"
"Pierre the Pirate!"
"Indians!"

The children all made their hopeful suggestions. Today Luke told the children about 'Cowboy Hank and the Cattle Rustlers' as he spun the tale, breathing was the only sound the children made. They listened to his every word. Their excitement spurred the story forward.

After the story, Maggie passed out her special gift of oranges to the eager hands around her. While they ate their rare delicacy, Luke let the children who had made him pictures describe them.

Tommy stood by his side "I made the sky all grey and cloudy with a big fat circle moon, and there's a island with lots trees and a treasure chest full of gold cups and diamond necklaces. There's two pirates and they is really happy cause they found it. And there's a big pirate ship with lots of sails and a Jolly Roger flag and one of the pirates has got a red and blue parrot and ones got a wood leg!"

To Luke this masterpiece was better than any of the paintings at the museum.

## 2

    The couple said good-bye to the children and got into Maggie's car. The wind hit Luke's face as they drove and as always compared it to flying with Sabatok. Maggie was talking about the upcoming election. Luke listened with only half his mind. He knew her opinions and let her rant about Herbert Hoover and how we must elect Roosevelt. He didn't disagree, but his passion for politics was not as hot as hers. They reached his home and he kissed her good bye in the car.

    Luke guessed that if he were human he might be tired from the long day, but his energy was not easily drained. He placed his precious new drawings in a box he kept for them and placed it under his bed. He strolled from room to room of his large house stopping to examine the various sculptures he had acquired. His hands ran over the cool marble of female figure. She seemed to stand on the edge of a cliff with the wind whipping back her long hair and dress. She was searching for something or someone. Luke imagined her forlorn lover ship wrecked and left on a distant island.

    The thought depressed him. He moved on to his beautiful onyx mustang in another of the rooms of his empty house. What would it be like if he took Peter into his home? Raised the boy and gave him everything he could ever want? But logic answered him back. Peter would eventually see his dark unnatural state, and he would either have to bring him over or abandon him. He could do neither. He would never consider condemning a soul to live off the life of others.

    He trusted himself only another few months at this house. He had four homes in four states. He stayed for five years at a time in each and then moved on to another. In a few months he would move to his Kansas City house. Tomorrow he would have one of the lawyers hire a house cleaning crew to prepare it for him. He would begin breaking ties with his friends and eventually he would do the heart breaking task of saying good-bye to the children at the children's home.

He used to feel such solace in his solitude, now that it threatened to last forever he wasn't sure he could bear it.

He decided he needed to walk. He headed out the door at moved at uncanny speed until he reached some population. He reached his mind out and explored those around him. His heart was heavy and lonely. He searched person after person until he found the particular kind he wanted.

There it was a wicked woman, plotting the murder of her husband. She held a bottle of poison in her hand and prepared to pour it into her husband's stew. She was angry, spiteful and greedy. Luke heard her plans to spend insurance money. He even knew this was not the first husband who would die at her hands.

Once again he moved with his other worldly speed until he reached a run-down tenement building. He entered and the smell of dirt and human waste filled his nostrils. He went to the door that separated him from Mrs. Polanski who stirred a stew and waited for her soon to be dead husband to arrive. He opened with a bang and he enjoyed her shock. She turned around expecting her husband or perhaps the police but instead she looked into the face of ravenous rage. She had only a moment to register his face and she saw nothing else.

Luke walked down the street feeling the shame of his detestable act and coming off the high of the delectable blood. The bliss of the fountain faded and was replaced again with his own emotions, now with added shame and fury at himself for giving in to the temptation again.

No matter what good deeds he performed, no matter how much of his fortune he gave away, it didn't change what he was. People thought he was a kind philanthropist. He was a murderer. Nothing would change it. There was no hope.

# 3

Luke walked through the Kansas City house with his new housekeeper walking next to him as he explained her job to her.

Vera was thin and quick and paid close attention to her new boss. "Excuse me Mr. Logan, there's no food at all in this kitchen, will you make me a list of what you like and don't like, and I'll get groceries as quickly as possible. I think they should have done that for you when they were preparing the house."

"I'm a bachelor Vera, I eat my meals out. There's really no need to get groceries."

"It's not healthy for a young man to eat out every day, especially every meal. You tell me what you like and I'll make sure you at least eat something that's good for you."

"Fine, get the staples. I like everything. Buy what you like. I'll make sure you have a budget for the kitchen. But cooking is not why I hired you. I just need you to keep the house clean and my clothes clean. Keep it presentable. It's a large house, so it's a large job."

"Young man, I mean you no disrespect, I raised two sons and two daughters, and I can't help but see you're barely more than a boy yourself. I'll be happy to keep your house and you will never have to concern yourself for anything. I'm a good housekeeper, but I'm a mother first. It'll hurt me if I think you're eating all your meals in restaurants and parties. Beside's that, you are one person. I doubt it will take me all day to clean the house. I'll have plenty of time to cook."

Luke immediately liked the woman and decided he could eat a few meals to make her feel better.

Luke bought a car and hired a driver. He had fallen in love with riding in automobiles. The wind flowing through his hair reminded him of flying. The speed reminded him of riding Bessie. Although he wasn't able to drive the car, he enjoyed the power of it.

He found the Logan Meats run soup kitchen and volunteered. They were surprised to see such a privileged young man willing to help out the large needy community, especially a blind man. They were impressed that rather than wallow in self-pity he worked hard to improve the lives of those around him.

He next located the children's home and offered his services there. He was not welcomed in at first. So he offered the references of Mrs. Foster and her boss Mr. Tomlinson and the couple Mr. and Mrs. James reluctantly agreed to let him come in on Sunday afternoons to spend time with the children.

# 4

Isaac, Luke's driver dropped him off at the park and Luke walked along the new path created by workers hired in Roosevelt's 'New Deal'. He noticed a man walking some feet behind him who was watching Luke walk along swinging his little walking stick in front of him. The man kept his attention on Luke for a while. He wondered where Luke had come up with using the walking stick and thought he could use a white cane. Luke listened in surreptitiously, he'd never heard of a white cane. His curiosity was aroused. He slowed his pace, found a bench and sat down.

His follower decided to approach. "Excuse me, my name is Dr. Gudd. I couldn't help but notice you're blind and well, I have some experience with blind patients. I admire your ingenuity with the walking stick. We have something that may be of interest to you. Not only would it help you ambulate more freely the way your walking stick does, but also it would offer you protection as a symbol to others that you're blind."

"I'm Luke Logan." Luke held out his hand in greeting and the doctor took it. "I'd be interested in hearing about it. What is it?"

"Can you meet me at my office? I'll tell you all about it and even demonstrate its use for you."

"Sure. Yes, that sounds fine Dr. Gudd."

**The doctor handed Luke a small slip of paper.** "This is my name, telephone number and the address of my office. Can you come at noon tomorrow?"

"Sure. Thanks" Luke tucked the slip of paper into his coat pocket, got up and continued his walk.

At the doctor's office the next day, Luke sat and listened to the man describe the 'white cane'. Luke held the slender stick in his hand it was longer than his stick and Dr. Gudd explained that this would actually allow him faster movement. He explained the stick was white and it alerted motorists and pedestrians alike to the condition of the user. He told him that several years earlier Peoria Illinois had made a law granting the right of way to blind pedestrians using the cane. Similar laws were being made throughout the country.

He showed Luke how the cane was commonly held diagonally in front of the user. Luke tried it and decided he liked his own use better for free walking but when he was being led by the doctor the diagonal hold worked better. He was really impressed with the cane.

The doctor also then handed Luke a large booklet of heavy papers. "This is a brief history of the cane, a list of agencies such as The Lions Club that promote its use and tips and such to use it."

Luke held the booklet but doubted he would ask anyone to read it for him. "I think I'll let you keep this. I can't think of anyone that I would ask to read it to me. Besides I can contact you if I have questions."

"This is in braille. Don't tell me you don't read braille! I hope I don't offend you but you seem to be an educated man, why wouldn't you have learned braille. I mean I would guess by your ease of movement and the depth of your eyes you've been blind for most of your life."

Normally he would have told a stranger he'd been blinded only a few years ago, after completing school, but this man knew blindness too well. He could see by the size of Luke's under used eye balls that it had been many years. Luke had only heard of braille occasionally and had never really thought of learning it. It wouldn't have helped him on the ranch and now although he owned a huge company, he didn't run it himself.

"I've never learned it." Was all he chose to answer.

"Well then, would you like to learn?"

"Yes, that would be great. Thank you."

And so Luke began to learn to read again. He now entered the modern world of blindness. Luke also decided to get a pair of glasses to shield his ugly useless eyes from the stares of others.

# 5

Luke was walking from the children's home to a diner to meet his friend Leslie for dinner. Leslie was a tailor. He and Luke had met at a fundraiser and become fast friends. He suddenly sensed the void that meant another vampire was nearby. He stopped his walk. He searched the minds of other pedestrians but none told him who the vampire was or even that they were aware of the creature. Luke pin pointed it to a tree. It couldn't be Sabatok then, he would have walked amongst the people.

The fact that the vampire hid in a tree suggested that it didn't have good intentions. Luke started his walk again. The vampire followed from tree to roof top keeping his pace.

Luke and Leslie had nearly finished their meals.

"You're distracted Luke" said the tailor.

"I'm sorry, you're right. I just have something on my mind."

"Do you want to talk about it?" sa c Leslie feeling concern for his friend.

"No, I'm sorry. So you were saying that you could make coats for each of the children at the home. You can do that for me by Christmas?"

"Oh yes! No problem." I've even hired a new man. Do you want them all the same or different styles and colors?"

"Umm you choose the fabrics, colors and styles, that's not my forte. Make sure they don't look like uniforms and make them bright. Children should have bright things."

Dinner was finally over, Luke hadn't bothered eating much of his in his preoccupation. He had listened to the empty space of the vampire throughout the meal and it had stayed on top of the diner, waiting for him.

Isaac waited outside with the car where he'd agreed to meet Luke. He jumped out to open the door for Luke. Luke thanked him absently and stepped inside. The vampire followed him home.

When he arrived home, Luke told Isaac he wouldn't need him until tomorrow and please enjoy the rest of his evening. He went inside and sensed Vera upstairs. He rushed up the stairs and asked her to leave.

She protested but he finally talked her into going home and hour early.

Now he was alone in the house. He wondered if he should be preparing for battle or if the enigmatic creature would just keep watching him from a distance. Why would a vampire just watch him? He'd spent a brief amount of time with several vampires throughout the years. Some he liked, some he didn't care for at all. He was tense and waited by the front door. Then he decided he would end this now.

He opened the wide front door and called out for the predator to show itself.

Suddenly Celeste's musky scent filled the air. She didn't say a word. Her long nails streaked across Luke's face cutting four parallel gouges from eye to jaw.

He moved to kick her, but his leg only moved through the empty air.

"Why are you here Celeste? You're not welcome!"

"I hate you!" She screamed

Luke grabbed her by her throat and squeezed. She kicked at him and her superior ancient strength won out as he was forced to release his grip as his broken legs refused to support him. Her breath was heavy and fast and he knew she was hurting as well. He reached out to her and found an ankle. He yanked her leg hard and pulled it out from under her.

There was a sudden sucking of air and there was a third vampire in the room. Sabatok grabbed Celeste from the floor and with a low growl twisted her head and snapped her neck. She fell lifeless to the marble floor. It was over. She had just shown up and Luke would never know why. Now she was dead.

"Drink." Sabatok ordered. His large wrist was at Luke's mouth. Luke obeyed and then gritted his teeth as the bones knitted back together again. She was gone that quickly. He had spent so many years with her and now she was gone. Was it his fault? Did he have to add her death to the long list he took blame for? If not for her he would most likely have died all those years ago after escaping the thieves. Yet, she had lied to him, misled him and caused him to become a killer.

Luke wasn't sure what he felt about her death but he could actually feel her absence from his soul. He'd never realized before that he could feel a piece of her. In fact now he realized that he could feel a bit of Sabatok on his soul as well.

"I can feel it, her death, I mean. If she had died anywhere, I would have known it."

"Yes" said the older vampire. "Because she was your maker you were connected. If she made any others you have a little connection to them as well but not very strong."

Luke searched his spirit and found one little presence small and pulsating but nothing else. "I feel one and you as well. We're connected." He considered the other vampire. Was it a man, a woman, older or younger, insane like Celeste or lost like Luke had been?

"I've given you blood a few times. The first time to save your life, twice to increase your strength and teach you, and of course this time to heal you. I feel you too. If you concentrate, you can call me, and I you. We can always find each other through this connection. Let's clean up and go find a party. You need to drink."

Luke wondered if he should mourn Celeste but he would be lying if he did. It felt evil to go have a good time one the same night as his long lost maker had died. He was after all an evil creature. Sabatok had just saved his life. He decided to go have a good time with his dearest friend.


One of Luke's favorite luxuries was his big bath tub. He soaked in hot soapy water and let everything that happened wash out of him.

After he got out of the tub, Sabatok decided he was going to enjoy a soak. He spent over an hour in the tub and got out smelling of roses.

The two men dressed in tuxedos. Luke suddenly realized he had no driver. Sabatok had never bothered learning to drive. Luke was not going to fly to a party. He went to the telephone and ordered a taxi.

Sabatok stayed for three days. Vera thought Luke's uncle was a wonderful charming man. But he did keep his nephew busy.

Sabatok even helped out in the soup kitchen. Luke enjoyed the reactions of the other volunteers and the indigent as they met the large man dressed in formal stiff clothes passing out spoons and napkins to whom ever needed them. He had to hold back laughter when one woman and her child came in and the child decided to follow the huge vampire form table to table asking incessant questions.

# 6

When Sabatok left, Luke went to one of his favorite spots, the art museum. He had no one with him to describe anything, he just sat in the center of a display room. People passing might have thought he was meditating. He concentrated on that pulsating spot in his soul. He followed a thin wisp of pulse out of his body and across the state and further. It ended and he thought about the surroundings. He knew he was in a large city on the coast. He recognized New York. The other vampire suddenly realized he was there. He couldn't tell what or who but he knew something was there. Luke drew back to himself quickly. He knew the other vampire was a man. He knew he was in New York but he also sensed malice. He hoped the other vampire didn't know about the connection.

Now he reached out to Sabatok, in moments he found his mentor in his beloved Istanbul. The connection was clear and obvious. He felt Sabatok acknowledge him, almost give him a mental hug. He gave him a mental hug back and came back to himself again.

"Can I help you?" spoke a lovely voice

"Oh yes, I was just getting ready to find a guide. Do you work here?"

"Yes sir, I'm new. My name is Loretta. I'd be happy to take you on a tour. Are you aware of the prices?" She said

"Yes, take me to the front desk and I'll pay and we can get started."

He could easily have gone to the front desk himself. He came to the art museum often. But a woman felt much safer once she thought he was helpless.

"Oh, I didn't realize you're blind. I'd be happy to take you on a complimentary tour." She practically tripped over herself in apologies.

"No, Miss. I'll pay and I know it will be money well spent."

"It's Mrs. Jackson. I'm Mrs. Charles Jackson, but you can call me Loretta."

They went on their tour and he listened to her describe the paintings, including histories and other facts. He normally preferred his friends or art students he hired to take him because they didn't just repeat the spiel the museum had them memorize. But Loretta Jackson went off script for him, delving into the colors and shading of each painting as well as the style including the facts from the spiel.

Although Luke really couldn't remember what the colors looked like, he could still imagine the paintings with his own made up colors. He didn't know if his red was the same as the real red or closer to yellow. But he remembered green was grass and trees and blue was sky and ice. It was more than someone telling him 'this is a blue flower in a yellow vase' It was the way they said it. Someone might describe the same painting as "a single blue lily in a slender yellow vase, with the sun lighting it from and angle" or perhaps someone might say 'a lonely blue lily in a small vase on a red velvet cloth. The room is dark except for a shaft of light touching the flower."

He learned about the person describing as much as he learned about the painting. Most of them started out wondering why a blind man would care about paintings but ended having enjoyed the experience as much as he had.

The museum was currently showing a Max Ernst exhibit. Loretta apparently didn't appreciate surrealism. She didn't know how to describe the paintings. What she managed to describe was stilted and confusing. Luke decided he was going to have to hire an art student and come back another time. Surrealism was difficult to describe for anyone and Luke was glad to move onto a different exhibit. He much more enjoyed her descriptions of the romantic paintings. She lost herself in describing the dramatic scenes.

Then came the sculptures. He longed to touch them but the museum wouldn't allow it. So he listened to the descriptions similarly.

For sculptures he liked galleries, because the artists were there and wanted to sell their work. They were eager for people to appreciate it. They often jumped at the chance to let Luke 'see' the statues.

# 7

Luke leaned in to kiss Shelley Brightman on the neck. She enjoyed the nibble and moved her head so he could kiss her again. "Come on Miss Brightman we should get to the concert." Luke kissed her just once more and stood up to encourage her to leave the cozy corner of the restaurant so they could walk to the theater for the symphony concert.

As he walked arm in arm with the shallow socialite, he felt a passerby judge the couple with absolute disdain. He let Shelley lead him to his seat as his attention found the mind of the critical observer. He found a middle aged man accompanied by an older one. As he delved he discovered they were both priests and they were talking about the disgusting behavior of the couple at the private table.

Luke was disgusted that they had disregarded his privacy and that they so openly discussed his behavior. There was nothing wrong with a little kissing. People did much more than light kissing nowadays. He had done more than just kiss her neck, but not even she was aware of that small fact,

Humph! Christians! They had no real love as far as he could tell. God had some special love for them apparently since he protected them from this curse, but Luke couldn't tell why. They seemed one huge judgmental mass of hypocrites.

After the concert, Shelley took Luke on a tour of New York City. He was visiting the huge city. He met her through the hotel concierge and had invited her to the symphony. Now she offered to show him the sights with hopes of snagging a rich husband. He let her show him around the city. He was slightly annoyed by the one dimensional social climbing vixen.

She was a terrible tour guide. She spent most of her time flattering him. He remembered to compliment her often enough through the evening.

While she talked more about herself than the city she was supposed to be showing him, he made plans for tomorrow.  He was going to find his vampire sibling and measure for himself if he ought to speak to him or not. At least he would try to learn more about him.

He would recognize him as a vampire but he wouldn't have to tell him they were connected.

Shelley finally tired of the 'tour' came to the realization that Luke had no plans to buy her gifts or invite her to his hotel. She told him she needed to get back home. He hailed a taxi and took her home then went back to his lavish hotel.

# 8

Luke left the hotel early the next morning. He sent out the tendrils of his mind to find the vampire. He walked steadily toward the creature covering miles of ground. He walked at a human pace, and kept the reach of his mind as light as possible. He didn't want to alert or alarm the other vampire.

As far as he could tell the other vampire had not yet noticed his presence. After three hours he came to a seedy broken down building. The souls inside were the tired despondent souls of broken impoverished men, some who would kill easily for the slightest gain. He found his sibling in the basement alone.

Luke entered the building and walked down the wobbly stairs to the dank smelling basement. One half of the area was filled with crates, and broken furniture. A maze of rooms and halls filled the other half. He found his way to a tiny back room and stood outside trying to assess the creature on the other side of the door.

Finally Luke raised his hand to knock on the door. It opened before he made contact, and an angry vampire spoke. "What? What do you want? Why are you bothering me?"

"May I come in?"

"You're Luke! Why did you come here? What do you want? How'd you find me?" Now he sounded terrified.

"You know me?" Luke asked still standing in the musty cramped hall

"She talked about you a lot. She hated you. She said she loved you." Angry again, he said "She loved me…" He trailed off, lost in thoughts or place.

The strange vampire was small and Luke had the impression he had been an old man he was turned. "May I come in?" He asked.

"This is my room, my stuff, mine."

"Let's go somewhere then. Please you know me, but I don't know you. I won't harm you. I just have some questions then, I'll leave you alone if you want me to."

"Walk, yes OK. She's dead..."

The vampire was not quite right in the head. Luke couldn't put his finger on the problem. He was definitely not sound. They walked but Luke often had to coax the geriatric to continue.

He found a modest hotel on a less poverty stricken block and rented a room where they could speak uninterrupted. He led the unstable little vampire to the room and to a small table and chairs.

"Tell me about yourself, what's your name? Who are you? Asked Luke.

"I'm her servant. Waiting for her to come back but she's not coming back. She's dead. I'm hungry."

"What's your name?"

"My name?" He thought for a moment "I think it might be Edgar. That seems right. There aren't many rats left. I don't like them."

Luke couldn't bring himself to want to help the man get blood. Let him eat rats. "Edgar." He said trying to get him back on track. "When did she bring you over?"

"I was about to jump off my building. I'd lost everything. She was next to me whispering to me that my money was gone, in the crash. I jumped, but she caught me. Somehow she was next to me then she was catching me and she took me to a cave. She killed me. She made me promise my life to her. She made me sleep, and when I woke up, I was her slave."

"Was it the stock market crash? Was it 1929?"

"Yeah, 1929 she told me it was cruel to let my family go on without me. My first blood was my granddaughter Amelia. She killed my wife, she killed all of them. They were gathered for my funeral and she killed all of them. Amelia wore the prettiest little dress it was white with little pink flowers embroidered on the edge. Catherine made it for her."

Luke was sick thinking of what had happened to the pathetic old man. No wonder he was so unstable. He'd been a slave for nearly ten years to a cruel soulless creature who had forced him to murder the child he loved most in the world. He'd loved money more. That had been his downfall. He almost felt sad enough to help him find blood.

"She was training me to kill you. I'm very hungry… She said I wasn't strong enough. She beat me but I loved her. YOU KILLED HER! I'm so hungry." He went from whispers to screaming and then to an unnerving calm from sentence to sentence. One moment he seemed afraid the next calculating. Luke doubted there was much left in his head to calculate anything.

"Why don't you hunt if you're hungry?"

"She told me to wait for her. Only hunt with her never alone."

"She's dead; she has no power over you anymore. You can hunt." Luke regretted saying it, now there would be more murders against him.

The old man lunged for Luke and grasped his neck. Luke took the weak hands off his neck and threw him across the room. "I could have helped you! You're pathetic! I can kill you Edgar very easily."

"Please don't! I'll do anything for you. Let me serve you. "He was begging him kneeling and grasping Luke's pant legs with his very dirty hands.

"I don't want a slave." Luke lifted the man of his knees and forced him to stand.

"I could be your servant. I would be good. I need someone. She ensured I would be weak by choosing me when I was already an old man. I can't be alone. I need someone to tell me what to do. I'm too weak in my body, mind and soul."

"You're weaker than me but you're still stronger than any human"

"I can't survive alone. If you won't let me be your slave, then kill me." He begged.

Luke had no desire to kill him and even less want of a slave or even a student. The unstable old man was not a companion he wanted. But he couldn't leave him to suffer. "I'll teach you to hunt without killing. Swear to me you will not take human life and I'll let you live." Luke didn't know another way to stop the old man from taking lives. Any life Edgar took would count against Luke.

"I swear it. I swear I won't kill a human, and I swear I will obey your every command as your devoted slave. You are my master. I am your humble servant."

"NO! How dare you? I told you I can't want you for my slave! I'm going to teach you my way of feeding without death and I'm going to leave you. I hope to never see you again!"

"Not a problem for you. When did you last see anyone?" He laughed as he spoke. Luke was sure that Edgar was insane. He supposed killing your granddaughter, then serving an abusive monster would break any mind, especially a weak one.

Luke ignored the comment. He wanted to get this teaching over and done with as quickly as possible. "All you have to do is get your prey close to you. Kiss them quickly and before they're aware bite and sip, kiss again. You can do that a few times a day and it'll be enough to sustain you." He hated this disgusting creature now. "Compel them if you need to, to tell them to forget or to be calm. Use your seeming fragility to get people to assist you. Pretend you need help walking. Follow me, I'll watch you try it. But first there's a rat in the corner, grab it so you won't be too hungry."

Luke left the room and the man obeyed him. Luke was sick to his stomach, since he knew Edgar now had no choice.

Edgar became very good at the nip and sip very quickly and Luke was sure it would be Okay to leave him.

Edgar depended on his ability to compel quite a bit, because he had no natural charm or logic. He would say bizarre things to people. He would quote from a novel he had read called *Dracula* by Bram Stoker. He would go in to take his drink and say "There is a reason why all things are the way they are." Or "I am all in a sea of wonders. I doubt; I fear; I think strange things, which I dare not confess to my own soul." Then he would go into fits of laughter.


Luke was ready to go home. He and Edgar were in the modest room Luke had rented. "I can get this room for you for longer if you want." It was much nicer than the hole Edgar chose to live in.

"No, it's not mine. I like my stuff. Let me come with you."

Luke had to choose his words carefully, first so he wouldn't give Edgar any commands and secondly so he wouldn't anger the unpredictable vampire. "I want to home alone. I don't want you with me. You'll be fine here."

"Let me come, I tell you about the cure."

"A cure for what?"

"A cure to THIS!" Edgar yelled, then in an almost sing song voice "I could tell you where to find it. The church has it."

"You're insane! You're staying away from me."

Luke left without further conversation.


The train ride home might have been pleasant for some people, but Luke was bored. He felt confined to his private compartment. He didn't bother to go to the dining car at meal times. He did go to the club car for cocktails. No one was aware that he sipped on their rich blood as they sipped on their libations.

He spent the boring solitary hours mulling over Edgar. He was clearly insane, and maybe he should have killed him when he asked. He loved an unlovable dead woman and ranted about impossible cures. He'd not only compelled victims to forget that he'd drunk from them but he'd compelled one woman to forget her own name. He was clearly out of his mind.

# 9

Luke left the children's home and told Isaac that felt like walking.

"Mr. Logan, You don't mean to walk home do you? That's nearly ten miles."

Of course, Luke realized it wouldn't be plausible for him to walk that distance on his own, so he changed his plans. "Give me an hour and meet me back here. I'll go home then. Go get a cup of coffee."

"Yes sir." Answered Luke's caring driver.

Luke walked from the children's home to the cathedral nearby. He didn't enter the large church. He stood outside and scanned the minds of those inside. He wasn't sure exactly what he looked for, but he looked anyway. Perhaps there was some cure. Luke knew that couldn't be true. But it was the tiniest hope, put far away in his heart. There were more people in the church than he had expected but realized most were priests and nuns. He spent a little time with each of them. One man prayed, another tried to convince himself he didn't need another drink. A woman spoke harshly to herself about her love of Father Madsen. Then he came across an evil man with horrible thoughts about an altar boy.

He was instantly furious. He doubted a religion that would put such evil in a high place could hold some antidote to his own malevolent condition. If they did, he suspected that they would hold it for their own profit.

"Mr. Logan!" came Isaac's voice. "I'm sorry but I was worried about you. You've been standing there stock still for about an hour and half. Are you OK? I was wondering if you're ready to come home."

An hour and half? Impossible! "I told you to go get a cup of coffee. Did you follow me?" He sometimes wished his human servants would follow his commands without choice.

The man swallowed hard. He wasn't sure what to say. "Sir I did go get coffee but then I saw you standing here when I drove by and, well, you don't look well. And you haven't moved even a little bit." Luke could feel the man's very real concern.

"Fine, yes, I'll come home. I'm fine, just thinking." He walked to the car and Isaac quickly opened the door and helped him in. Luke swallowed back his irritation.

Vera was tripping over herself with worry. Luke ignored her concern and went up the stairs to take a bath so he could be alone. He could clearly hear Isaac and Vera discussing him in hushed tones. They worried for the young man. He seemed so sad and angry since his return from his business trip. He had poured himself into his charity work.

"Do you know he hasn't had a single meal at home in the past two weeks?" asked Vera.

"He hasn't been eating out that much either. I suppose he eats at the parties and maybe at the soup kitchen. There is something very wrong with him."

"He doesn't have his mother and father to look out for him anymore. He needs us to step in and care for him. He needs someone. He is so independent, and sometimes so careless about himself. I don't care what that boy says, I am not going to let him make himself sick." With that Vera went to the kitchen and made a dinner that Luke hadn't ordered.

When he was out of the bath and dressed for bed. She ordered him downstairs to eat the dinner she had cooked. "You are not looking well. I made you a nice hearty meal and young man, you are going to eat it."

Although Vera was talking and she kept talking through the entire meal, Luke heard Melba's voice speaking through this woman. He missed that family. He realized he had two people willing and waiting to step into a family role for him. So he finally gave in and let them be who they wanted to be for him.

"Thank you Vera. This is delicious. I'm sorry I haven't felt myself lately. Can you please make sure you have a nice lunch made for me every day? Don't worry about the weekends of course. I think this dinner was just what I needed to help me feel better." Luke hugged the relieved woman, kissed her cheek and went to listen to the radio in the den.

As he half listened to the program, he ran his hand over the onyx mustang. Her power, her freedom her joy reverberated through him as he imagined himself on her back racing through the open country, the sun on his face and Melinda waiting for him at home.

# 10

Luke was enjoying the afternoon with Sophie Monroe. She had recently graduated college and had not yet settled down to marry anyone, much to her parent's consternation. She was smart, self-assured and funny. He'd met her after hiring her to guide him around the art museum. Her descriptions had been sparkling and hot-blooded.

She had talked Luke into taking a pottery class. The class was great. He became the artist. Everyone but Sophie was surprised by his talent. She told him she could tell by the touch of his hands that he would be a master.

He loved the feel of the wet clay. He loved the way his slightest pressure changed its shape. He had a natural intuition on how to create the object he wanted. He could tell that people were sincere in there admiration for his work.

Sophie looked at his latest piece, a slender urn that blossomed like a flower at the lip. "I think after this is baked it should be painted deep plum then glazed."

Luke laughed a little. "I trust your artistic eye. It's better than both mine together."

Sophie laughed along with him. And he appreciated her all the more. They had been friends for five months now. He could picture spending years enjoying her company. But he was very close to having to move to another city. To ask her to come with him would mean marrying her, or worse, telling her and therefore turning her. He had no intention of ever bringing another soul to this curse.

Vera had insisted on making dinner for Luke and Sophie. Luke could hear her plotting to marry them off. She thought it was a great tragedy that her young boss lived the lonely life of a bachelor. He was such a handsome, kind man and she was sure that having a woman in his life would improve his moodiness. She could tell his moodiness was not only due to loneliness but also pride. Anytime he felt his independence was infringed upon or though someone pitied him he couldn't help but be grouchy.

Luke listened to her thoughts. She was a sweet woman. "I suppose you'll want me to pretend I made this sophisticated meal? It smells amazing. What is it?"

"Oh, Mr. Logan! She knows you well enough you've never stepped foot in the kitchen except to steal cookies. I made roasted lemon chicken stuffed with carrots and squash. I have real roasted potatoes, not the powdered ones, and I made a small loaf of bread. It's not fancy, just good simple home cooking. She's a nice down to earth girl. She isn't impressed by caviar and escargot. No, you'll catch her by being yourself without all the fuss and tuxedos."

"I'm not trying to catch her Vera. I'm sorry to tell you, I am a life-long bachelor and Sophie and I are just good friends."

Once Sophie arrived, Vera set the table and left the pair alone. As usual the conversation flowed easily and could get deep.

"Sophie, do you think good deeds can make up for bad ones?"

"I don't know. I guess it depends, I mean if you steal from someone, they often lose more than just the value of what was stolen. They also lose trust. Thievery can snowball into great financial loss. So I don't know. A good deed can snow ball too. I guess it depends on the size of each deed. I think a good deed has to be way bigger than the bad one to make up for it."

"I wonder if some acts can be made up by anything. Do you think there are some people so bad they're beyond redemption?"

"Wow, I think that God is good and if a person is generally good, He knows it, and He lets them into paradise."

What if a person wants to be really good but has done some really horrible things? What makes the difference between a good man and a bad one? How many sins is one too many?"

"Luke, you are a good man. I doubt you've ever done anything so bad you couldn't make up for it. You are the kindest, most charitable person I know. And doesn't wanting to be good mean something? I mean a bad person wouldn't want to be good would they? And you do more than want to be good, look at all the good you do."

"Thanks Sophie. You are as wise as your name implies." He decided to end the conversation. He couldn't reveal his dark soul to her.

She laughed her throaty genuine laugh and they moved on to other topics

# 11

Luke sat in the law office awaiting the lawyer, a Mr. Carter to come into the room. They had explained to him that through long tradition and laws his fortune was now even bigger since he was inheriting Celeste's immense wealth.

"What about Edgar Burrows? He was made by her as well, she duped him out of his money the day she took him and lied to him."

"Whether you like it or not, He was her slave and now he's yours. The money is yours. These are ancient and complicated laws."

"How did you know he was my slave? I didn't tell anyone. I don't want a slave and I didn't choose him to be my slave."

"We are more than human here. We have our ways. Constantine, Carey and LeRiche has its share of vampires on staff but we also have others. I in fact was once an angel. I was cast out of heaven along with many others. We are powerful. We have ways of knowing things that are beyond you. Yes, there are humans but they would never be entrusted the details you prefer to be kept private. So let's just say anything of importance that happens involving your money, your vows, or your soul, we become aware of it."

Luke thought to ask about some of Edgar's curious statements but decided not to. Was Carter saying he was a demon? If Demons were real, didn't that mean god was real? He wondered how much of his thoughts Mr. Carter was privy to.

"Don't worry Mr. Logan your thoughts are your own and private. Reading your mind is not one of my powers." Mr. Carter said in his cryptic way. "We do have some vampires on staff that share your gift for telepathy, but none sir can read your mind. Your thoughts are yours alone."

"Mr. Carter," Luke said, "I'd like to give Edgar Burrows five million dollars. Please arrange it."

"Okay no problem. Now will you need me to prepare your San Francisco home? I believe, the last time we spoke you mentioned moving by August. It's November now."

"I've decided to stay in Kansas City for a while longer. I'll let you know when I'm ready to move."

"Yes sir. I'll have Carol show you out." Ben Carter stood up and left the room.

# 12

Luke worked a large block of clay in his strong hands. He formed it into beautiful Bessie, probably long since gone. He cut away clay leaving the shape of her muscled body. He ran the ribbon cutter along the top of her and her shape began to emerge from the heavy clay. His hands remembered every contour of her. How many times had he moved the brush over her hair the same way he now moved the cutting tool over the sculpting clay.

Sophie had stopped working on her own statue, a bust of Luke, to watch him perform his magic on the clay. She thought she'd never seen anyone take to molding clay as quickly as he had. She knew he would have talent because he loved art so well. But his aptitude for every sort of pottery and sculpture they had tried so far was really spectacular.

Luke put the tools down and now finessed the clay with his fingers as he got her powerful back just right. He had to make the contour from her back to her neck just so. Her stance was a peaceful one. She seemed just about to nuzzle Luke.

He picked up the small cutting tool and very carefully carved her face.

Sophia watched, Luke's bust long forgotten beneath her hands and a tear rolled down her face at the beauty of the horse.


"I have a surprise for you Luke. It's about an hour's drive from here. Are you ready?"

"Sure, am I dressed OK?" He purposely stayed out of her mind so he could enjoy the surprise with her. It was harder than he thought because it proved how much he depended on others thoughts of the world to shine a little light on his darkened path.

"Actually, you should go wear something casual and sturdy."

"You go up and pick something for me."
She did and soon he was dressed very comfortably in a pair of jeans.

The car had travelled for about an hour and was starting to slow down Sophie was full of excitement. "Okay closes your eyes!"

Luke laughed, "Okay if it'll make you feel better."

They got out of the car and the beautiful scent of grass, dirt, hay and manure met Luke. He half expected to hear Ike calling out a greeting.

Sophie took Luke's arm and led him to a man who introduced himself has Mr. Tex James.

Sophie could barely hold her excitement. "We're going horseback riding!"

Tex looked at the couple, a blind boy and a rich girl. "Have either of you ridden before?"

"Yes." They both answered.

Luke was surprised to find out she had ridden. "We used to go on all sorts of vacations. My father is obsessed with the Old West and so whenever it was his turn to plan the vacation, I invariably ended up the back of a horse."

"Kind of the same here, but it's been a long time." I'm more than ready."

Tex wasn't convinced but watching them both mount the horse helped. And once they'd ridden for ten minutes he agreed that they could ride without a guide.

The ranch was set up so that tourist could ride trails and view nature as the city lives didn't allow. They rode at a casual pace. Luke liked his horse. A mare named Sugar, she had a calm demeanor He had a feeling she was the horse saved for children and timid new riders, she was so very calm.

"I'd love to run a little, is there somewhere we can run?"

"Sure follow me." And she was gone. Luke loved that she either forgot he was blind her didn't think it was the hindrance so many others did. He could easily decide to fall in love with this girl. He enjoyed the friendship much too much for that.

And they were off. Sugar seemed happy to break out of her usual slow pace. Wind blew through Luke's hair. The strong horse ran without restraint and he felt the rare freedom along with the wonderful memory of his long lost past. He was his onyx mustang at this moment.

# 13

The house was transformed into a winter wonderland for the big Christmas party. Vera was attending the party but didn't like the idea of the caterers in her kitchen or the party planning staff crawling over her house.

Luke told her to relax and just let them work. "Go home and get dressed up so Rick can show you off. I want my family enjoying the party not working at the party."

In addition to the orphans, who were the guests of honor, Luke had invited the volunteers and some regular attenders at the soup kitchen, Isaac and his family, the staff of the museum, several art students, The crème of society and of course Sophie and her family. The large house buzzed with activity as people prepared the house for the party.

Luke had hired one of the soup kitchen volunteers to play Santa Claus and pass out gifts to the children. The robust and friendly Joe Stevens was born for the job.

A small band would play music and there was even a place for dancing. Even Luke was looking forward to the festivities.


"Come dance with me Luke. I feel so magical." Sophie took Luke's arm and they walked to the dance floor. Luke had never been a dancer, ranch life didn't lend itself to dance lessons, and in his vampire life he hadn't bothered to do much besides the slow close dancing that made nip and sips so easy. He was relieved when the music slowed and he held Sophie in his arms and moved to the rhythm of the music.

While they danced they talked. Sophie looked at the children and Luke felt her heart pang for them. She especially noticed a small girl with dark curls and big eyes. She wondered if her own daughter might look like that, or would she have Luke's fair coloring?

Luke stopped moving cold. "I need to check on the gifts and I think Santa will be coming soon. I'm so sorry to leave you in the middle of a dance."

Sophie was annoyed at his lack of manners. She had long ago accepted that Luke had certain eccentricities. Gift giving was far more important to him than being a gentleman and finishing a dance. She gave a heavy sigh and let him go. He was who he was.

Luke went the direction of the room where some of the wrapped toys were being put into large sacks for distributing. The other gifts were already piled high under and around the giant tree. He didn't make it to the room though. Sophie's mother was talking to Mrs. Lancaster the wife of the wealthy owner of a steel company. "They've been dating for some time. He had been planning a sabbatical but put it off for over a year. I think he didn't want to leave Sophie. I'm sure he's proposing tonight and after the wedding, the sabbatical will be a honeymoon." She spoke in the hushed tones reserved for gossip.

"Oh! Do you really think so? How marvelous! You know I've heard he's one of the wealthiest men in the country. And," she added with a bit of disgust, complimentary words meant to insult. "He actually goes to the soup kitchen and mingles with the vagrants himself. He even insisted some of those unfortunates come to his party."

"Well I know he gives a great deal of money to charities. Do you know he even paid for an entire new building for the art program at the university? I expect when the gifts are brought out for the children, the last gift will be for Sophie and it will be a ring and a proposal."

"Well, that is just marvelous. It's a shame he's blind. Such a waste, that your daughter's beauty is wasted on him. He could've dated Susan Thompson. She's so plain, only her father's bank account will attract a husband for her."

Luke walked away into the outdoors for a breath of fresh air. He needed to think. He needed to calm down. Once out of sight of the party guests he walked with his supernatural speed without concern of where he was.

Luke stood over the dead and bloodless priest. As the ecstatic high slowly came down, he realized what he had done. Rapture was replaced with guilt. The lightness of his soul was made heavy by the burden, and heavier still that he didn't remember initiating the act. He tossed the corpse into a furnace, and sped home.

He walked in the door. The party continued but Sophie found him. "Darling! Where have you been? I've been worried, so has Vera."

"I'm sorry, I had to get some air. I had to think. We need to talk but not tonight I don't want to ruin the party for anyone else."

"That doesn't sound good. Okay we'll talk tomorrow. You were gone walking for nearly an hour. You know you could have said something. We were worried."

He spoke low and slow holding his anger in check. "I am more than capable of taking a walk alone. I told you I needed to think. I guess it was rude to leave the party, but I am after all eccentric and people expect me to do unusual things occasionally" He left her bewildered at the door.

The gifts from the bag had been passed out and Santa now gave out the packages from under the tree. The joy and hopeful excitement in the room finally began to do its work on Luke.

Sophie was happy to see his dark mood lifted. She worried about whatever might be bothering him. But she didn't hold it against him. He was too good a man to let one moody moment change her feelings for him.

Luke noticed the only people disappointed by lack of marriage proposal that evening were Sophie's parents. A woman's longing for a child did not have to translate to instant need for marriage.

He decided regardless it was time to start getting ready to move to San Francisco. He had let himself get too close to happiness and he didn't deserve it.

# 14

The art gallery was showing a new artist and both Sophie and Luke were excited to go see his work. When they arrived Sophie was thrilled. "Oh! Luke it's all cowboys and western!"

They strolled from painting to painting. They admired a large canvas and Sophie described it." It's a grassy empty plain. The grass has a purple hue and its bend over in the wind. The sun is setting and the sky is all oranges and purples and the higher up it goes the darker it is. The very highest part of the sky is a dark dark blue almost black. In the middle of the plain is a cowboy with his back to us. His hands are both holding six shooters but they're just hanging by his side. His head is bowed down, just a little. He seems so forlorn. There is a hint of someone lying on the ground in the distance. I suppose it's a dead cowboy. You can see the tips of his boots and a knee mostly."

"It's beautiful." Said Luke

"Thank you," said a quiet man it's one of my favorites, and I quite enjoyed your description Miss…"

"Monroe." Sophie shook the gentleman's hand "I'm Miss Sophie Monroe and this is my friend Mr. Luke Logan."

I'm Mitch Roberts. I'm happy to make your acquaintance. This is one of my favorite pieces and you did a beautiful job of describing it. Would you mind if I joined you while you look at the rest of my work?"

"We'd love it" Said Luke. "We would enjoy the artist's insights."

Mitch Roberts was a little older than Sophie and according to her opinion a very handsome strapping man. His appearance made one think of a western hero down to his boots and his leather vest.

Both Luke and Sophie enjoyed the man's easy sense of humor and unusual humility.

Mitch let Sophie describe the paintings and he thought she was spot on with her impressions. He liked her ease and joy, her insights and her intelligence. Her lovely dark long hair and delicate features added to her beauty but weren't the only things that defined it.

Sophie described another painting. "Everything has an amber hue because it's that magic hour between day and night, twilight. Dark against the amber of the background there is a cowboy leaning against a barren tree on what seems like a barren ground. He looks tired, and alone. He has so much on his mind. He seems heavy with it. It's sad and yet you can see he's strong and just taking a breather from everything. He's the only one who knows how much is weighing him down. Luke I don't know why but he reminds me of you. I think this is beautiful Mitch."

Luke offered to buy the *Lonely Hero* for Sophie as a gift but she opted to buy it herself.

Luke invited Mitch to dinner that evening and was very happy that the man accepted. He was also happy to find Mitch was just as attracted to Sophie as she to him. But neither moved on their feelings for Luke's sake. And Luke was the only one aware of the mutual esteem.

Over a steak dinner the three got to know one another.

"I would guess it's very rare for a blind man to love art the way you do, especially paintings. How did you come to like it so much? I mean, um... well you can't tell anything about the style the brushstroke, what is it you like?"

"A long time ago, I got to know an art student and she took me to a gallery. Her descriptions were so good. I just fell in love with viewing paintings through other people's eyes. I find I can see the same painting many times and it's different for me each time based on my company. It's also a great way to meet girls." He added the last in an effort to remind Sophie that they were casual and let Mitch in on the fact. "I also enjoy sculpture and I can enjoy that on a deeper level. I get the description as well as my own interpretation."

Sophie interjected "Luke is quite a good himself he's wonderful with clay."

Luke added that Sophie too was an artist and before long Mitch and Sophie were discussing art and Luke sat back and enjoyed quietly.

He formed the plan that he needed to get the two together. Sophie had begun to think of a future family with Luke in the role of husband. He could never be that for her, he needed to move someone else into that spot of her mind and Mitch seemed ideal.

Luke couldn't find anything bad about the guy. He wasn't lazy. He was honest, compassionate and down to earth. He really suited Sophie.

"We're going to a fundraiser for the children's Home next week, please joins us." Luke said.

"Thank you that sounds great." Answered Mitch

"Sophie can you write out the information for him, please? I'll have a car pick you up at your home Saturday at seven, and I'll pay for the ticket."

# 15

Luke arrived home and felt Edgar lurking in the trees outside his house reminding him a little of Celeste. He made sure the house was empty then called the elderly vampire into his house. "Edgar, come in here!"

The strange little creature appeared suddenly.

"Edgar why are you here? Tell me the truth."

"Doctor, you don't know what it is to doubt everything, even yourself. No, you don't; you couldn't with eyebrows like yours." He was quoting Bram Stoker again Luke was sure.

"Edgar!" growled Luke

"You killed! You tell me not to kill but you do. You're a hypocrite!"

"I... you're right... I didn't mean to kill Edgar, it was an accident, he was an evil man, and my rage took over."

Quoting Bram Stoker again the vile geriatric said ""There are mysteries which men can only guess at, which age by age they may solve only in part." Then he went to the door. "I'm here so you'll be close by when you need to be. Follow me if you want to"

The insane vampire was gone and Luke chased as closely as he could. They came to palatial home on a hill several miles from Luke's own home. Inside several souls slept unaware of anything. One person lounged languorously in an upstairs room eating chocolates and drinking brandy. When Luke got closer he knew it was a woman. She was nearly drunk, and as apathetic as the worst of the very wealthy.

Edgar stood in a corner watching her, his breathing heavy. The woman had not sensed his presence. Then Edgar stepped forward and once again quoting his beloved Bram Stoker he said in a loud voice ""Take me away from all this Death."

The woman screamed and just as quickly Edgar was on her and drinking in a frantic manner.

Luke rushed forward "NO!" but the woman was dead.

Edgar pled again "Take me away from all this Death." And threw himself on Luke. Luke picked him up and he was a ragdoll. He threw him across the room and Edgar must have hit a mirror it crashed to the ground in a symphony. "Luke picked the pathetic and now very weak man up once again and tilted his head back to expose the throbbing jugular. Edgar didn't fight it. He gave himself over to his death. Luke drank deeply from him until Edgar was no longer. And it was Luke's fault, He added the lazy woman to his long list of victims as well. His evil was too great to ever be balanced.

Footsteps rushed up the stairs as servants awoke to the noisy commotion. Luke jumped out of the open window and left the scene to confuse the police who would surely be arriving soon.

Luke had never liked the little old man, but he had pitied him. Now he had killed him. He was disgusted with himself. He should have been merciful, he should have let him live. He could have found some way to release him from his slavery and let him live. To let him live meant to let him kill. Luke was a murderer. His list of victims was so great that he would never find redemption.

# 16

Mitch was working on a new painting and he'd asked Luke to pose. "Just stand in a comfortable way. Put your head down just a little. Point your nose to your left knee. Yeah that's it! Think about something like um… cattle rustlers or thieves, bad guys! Wait I'm gonna be making you a sheriff so think about bank robbers."

A shadow passed over Luke as Melinda squeezed his heart. She let it go and he got back to the business of posing. But Mitch was sensitive and noticed it.

"Did I say something? What's wrong?"

Luke knew that Mitch knew He had Sophie had been friends for about three years and that he was much too young to have lost a wife before that time, so in his story Melinda became his school sweetheart. He told Mitch the story of the bank robbery of course letting Mitch imagine it had happened to a young boy and his sweetheart going into the bank at the wrong time. Not a ranch owner and his wife, and his employees. But even the fictional version still hurt to tell.

Luke finished the tale and Mitch sat silently taking it in for a minute. He was so sad for Luke yet there was no pity in him. "I'm so sorry. You lost so much. It's terrible. If only she hadn't walked in just then. I'm so sorry. I bet Melinda was wonderful."

"She was vivacious and pretty and she loved pretty things. She was so social, it went perfectly with my shyness. We complimented one another. She would have been the perfect wife. In my heart, she is my wife and always will be."

"Luke, you are an amazing person. I can't imagine the pain you've been through. I've never met anyone that has impressed me the way you do, I doubt I will ever meet anyone that could come close"

The trio was supposed to be going to a jazz concert together, but Luke bowed out leaving Sophie and Mitch to go together. He could tell the two really liked one another's company. He had given each of them enough clues that he at least didn't think he and Sophie were in a relationship. He knew each of them had gotten the message. They were in love. He hoped they would get around to telling one another very soon.

He was preparing to bow out of their lives now, not just their dates.

Sophie, Mitch and Luke gathered for a farewell dinner at Luke's home. He would be leaving the next day for a long sabbatical, so Mitch and Sophie both earnestly believed.

"I have a gift for you Luke, but, it's a gift that I plan on keeping and you'll have to visit me whenever you want to enjoy it." Said Mitch

"That sounds like a great present. What is it?" Luke already knew that Mitch had brought a large canvas into the house and it sat on an easel covered with a sheet.

"Sophie please, do me a favor and describe this painting to Luke."

Mitch whisked the sheet off the canvas and Sophie stared in awe for a minute before she began. "There's a cowboy with long blonde hair hanging loose. He's wearing a hat and his head his bent so you only see the bottom part of his face. His mouth is set in determination. I can see he has a plan and means to carry it out. He's very handsome. He's determined. There's something good about him. Maybe the way the light shines off him. I don't know. Mitch, you are so talented. Anyway, He's standing, no he's walking out of a door that he's holding open with one hand. His other hand is holding a gun. In the window next to the door, you can just see a small reflection of a beautiful girl with golden hair done up under a fancy hat. She's really beautiful with a round face and green eyes."

"She's being held by some big hands. She's looking at the cowboy with complete confidence that he's going to rescue her. She loves him. Luke it's you. The cowboy Luke, it's you. And it's beautiful. Whatever you want to do in life, you manage to do. I've never seen you let anything stop you. You are the most generous, kind courageous man I've ever met. I'm going to miss you so much."

Luke took it all in.

Mitch was suddenly concerned. "Luke, you're bleeding! Here take my handkerchief."

"I'll go clean up and be right back. I hit my head just before. I guess I didn't realize it opened up." Luke rushed from the room to clean his tears from his face.

The couple was worried for their friend but since no other explanation seemed plausible they accepted that somehow an injury had waited an hour before bleeding.

When he got back, there was one more announcement. Sophie was happy but just a little nervous to tell her closest friend. "Mitch asked me to marry him, and believe it or not I accepted. I'm going to be Mrs Roberts. My mother won't know whether to be relieved that I'm finally settling down or disappointed that Mitch is not the heir of some family fortune. I have no problem living on an artist's means in a loft. It sounds like paradise to me."

"Let's drink to that!" Luke opened a bottle of champagne and the trio toasted to future happiness.

The next morning Luke boarded a train for San Francisco.

# 17

After only two years in San Francisco, Luke was restless and bored. He was tired of the same old thing. Working in soup kitchens and visiting orphans was fine, he'd added volunteering at the hospitals and retirement homes but still he felt that nothing good he did could make up for his countless murders.

He was tired of the shallow socialites, the uninspired art students that far out-numbered the inspired few, and bored rich businessmen.

He worked a piece of clay in his hands forming a free flying bird. He wasn't happy with the results though and couldn't bring his full attention to the task. He smashed the clay back into a ball and wrapped it to keep it from drying out. He washed his hands and tried to think of something to do. He could think of nothing and settled for taking a walk.

He let his driver take him to his favourite nature trail and told him to meet him in two hours. He walked along the well-worn trail, trying to figure out what it was he could do to change things or at least take a break from the monotony.

He finally decided on a long vacation. He would travel the world. It wouldn't matter how long he took. Perhaps he would visit The Louvre, and the Smithsonian. Maybe He would visit far off exciting places like Tahiti.


Luke made all the arrangements to ensure the housekeeping staff would be paid and the house still taken care of. He doubled his donations to the charities where he normally volunteered.

He booked a ticket on a ship and headed for France.

# 18

The ship and his accommodations were luxurious. He passed the time socializing and walking the ship, searching the minds of his fellow passengers. He felt no kinship with anyone. He'd never felt so lonely. Always in the past he'd been able to enjoy the company of the idol and vain elite. Now he put up with them only in order to nourish himself. He attended the meals on the large vessel to take up time.

He finally arrived in Paris after his long journey. In the decades since he'd last been here the smell had improved but the general mind set of the population felt similar. The city loved itself. Parisians consider themselves to be innovators and better than the rest of the world. He enjoyed letting them speak French to one another about him and then speaking French to them to take them down a peg.

Luke hired an art student to be his guide at The Louvre. Adele was a vivacious girl working her way through school. She was well versed in art history and had real appreciation for art of most types.

When she met Luke, she was at a loss as to how she was supposed to guide him through the museum, but he was paying very well so she was willing to give it a chance.

Luke explained what he wanted her to do. "Just describe the painting, tell me as you describe it how it makes you feel. Please remember that even if it's a painting that you've seen a hundred times, I've never seen it. Even if it's a famous painting please remember I have no idea what it looks like."

"I can do that."

"I'll meet you at nine AM sharp. Luke kissed Adele's diminutive hand and tasted her life without her knowledge.

Luke enjoyed the museum. When they saw the work of The Masters her awe of them translated into her descriptions. Luke longed to really see them himself. Even the building itself was artfully described.

When they left, Adele suggested that he let her show him a cathedral. He agreed and they took a cab to a cathedral she thought was beautiful and overlooked in the huge city.

The entered the building which wasn't as large as Luke had expected. Adele spoke in a reverent whisper as she described the gothic architecture and statues then moved to the many stained glass windows It really was beautiful.

He touched some of the smaller icons as she described not only what they looked like but what they meant to her. They were images of various saints. To him they meant nothing but to her, they held some power. He wondered if any of them held the power to cure him of his evil heart. He even considered asking her if she knew of a saint that healed vampirism. He dismissed the fleeting thought quickly. He knew the church didn't believe in his kind.

Luke paid for her taxi back home and took another to his hotel.

He started touring the cathedrals to see what it was about them that people like Adele found so impressive. He was impressed by their beauty but less impressed by the lavishness of most them, while hungry people begged outside their doors.

He thought this couldn't be the real church. He knew that the large catholic institutions were not the only kind of church. He bet the sort of church Melba had belonged to was more genuine than this. There were so many kinds of churches. Which one had the right dogma? Which one, if any had God's approval? Or did God sit in huge heavenly throne and laugh at them all for getting it wrong?

Luke moved from Paris to Barcelona, and then London, and Rome.  He explored Edinburg, Dublin and Moscow.

# 19

He was still bored, still restless and still lonely after almost two years of touring the world. He arrived back in San Francisco with a new idea to take up his time.

He opened an art gallery on a busy street. He hired a young man that he had come to like. He invited artists to show him some of their work and if he, his new staff member Joshua and anyone else present liked the work, he invited them to show it at his place.

The art now tended toward the Abstract and his empathy played a major role in his decisions toward or against showing an artist. If the person described a painting or a sculpture with indifference, he thanked the artist and sent them on their way. But when the art evoked emotion it improved his appreciation.

He now had something to do that he enjoyed. And the gallery offered a whole circle of friends. Sunday afternoons still belonged to the orphans, but the other six days of the week had Luke selling art, supporting artists and enjoying a social circle that wasn't made up of the stiff upper crust.

He planned parties to advance the careers of the painters, photographers and sculptors he showed. He opened a studio to teach the skills. Once a month the youngsters of the children's home came for free lessons.

Joshua was a gentle kind-hearted soul with a sense of humor as big as his heart. Luke found his descriptions were thoughtful and honest. His emotion and his words always matched whether describing a photograph or having a conversation. He was shy and Luke quickly discovered he didn't like the crowded parties.

So, Luke hired another person to host the parties in Joshua's stead. He found a colorful woman named Carmen who revelled in the details necessary to carry off an affair. She could throw a small intimate get together just as well as large loud shin dig.

## 20

Luke almost always let his lawyers handle all his bank business but some things had to be handled by him personally. He entered banks only when he had to and always with trepidation. Luke had to sign papers to continue to authorize Joshua to use the company account. Joshua accompanied him not only to sign his own papers but also to serve as Luke's eyes for the meeting.

The two entered the large branch and waited for Mr Jones to see them. Luke reached the fingers of his mind out as a natural habit, exploring the people around him. He found a man desperate for a loan, a child excited to be depositing money to her savings account, a man waiting patiently to cash a check and two men with dark plans.

The first man was making a mental list, perhaps even writing his observations, Luke couldn't know for sure. "One guard with a gun, safe within view, combination lock, door locks with a dead bolt…"

The second man made a similar list but his thoughts were more complex, "guard looks sleepy, I disarm him and Lou locks the doors, I keep the tellers and customers quiet, Lou collects the money, no alarm that I can see…"

Luke's heart froze in his chest. He could tell the plan wasn't meant for today. They were planning it for some other time. Could he stop them? Could he save some other person form losing their Melinda?

"Luke, are you Okay? You're pale as a ghost!" Joshua was very concerned for his boss.

"Yeah, I'm fine. I'm fine."

"No, I don't think you are! Let me get you a drink of water. The worried man was gone across the bank before Luke could respond and was back shortly with a small plastic cup of water.

Luke kept listening in on the second man. He searched the man for as much information as he could. Tony Russo had a wife at home and she had no idea that they were about to be rich. He'd been fired from his bakery job two days ago and she didn't know that either. He was an egotistical man who thought he was much smarter than anyone else around him. Lou was his sloth of a cousin.

The men left the bank.

"Joshua, I need to get some air, reschedule with Mr Jones and I'll meet you back at the gallery later." Luke didn't give Joshua a chance to answer. He left to follow the would-be bank robbers.

Lou and Tony discussed the plan as they walked, which proved to Luke that they were imbeciles. He caught up to them and pushed them into a narrow alley. He hit Lou hard on the head so the man fell unconscious then picked Tony up by his shoulders and held him against the brick wall.

"You deserve to die a slow and painful death." He meant to drink slowly and keep him alive for as long as possible to extend his suffering. But the blood felt so great that the man was dead in minutes. The blood rhapsody swirled through him.

Lou moaned bringing Luke out of his euphoria. Luke was on him in an instant and like an animal he sucked every drop of blood from the now deceased dolt. Luke basked in the high.

He threw the men like trash into a greasy diner dumpster, and threw a lighted match in. He walked away before the fire was big enough to attract attention.

As the high left him, he felt the remorse for his terrible deed. After a few blocks, he sensed Joshua as he franticly searched for his ill blind friend.

Luke wished for the ability to push his desires onto people the way any other vampire could. Joshua would have done exactly what he asked. But he couldn't be angry with the young man, he had really thought Luke was sick. It wasn't under estimating his ability that had made Joshua ignore his wishes it was concern.

He couldn't further shame himself by degrading his friend for his compassion.

"Luke! I found you. You look a little bit better. Are you Okay? Let's go back the car. I think you should go home and rest."

"I'm feeling much better. Thanks. Maybe you're right. Sometimes being in a bank reminds me of things I'd rather not think about." Luke said honestly.

"Really? Do you mind if I ask?" Joshua was careful and thoughtful.

"It's a long sad story. Take me home. Anita will make us some coffee and I'll tell you. I'll tell you because I know you won't pity me, and because you deserve to know why I was so upset. I don't know what it was, that brought it back to me, maybe someone wore the same cologne or something." Luke was much better at lying than most people.

He told a fictionalized version of the bank robbery, this time with his older brother John instead of Melinda. This time he was a thirteen year old boy putting his birthday money into a savings account and his brother John was impatiently waiting outside when the bank robbery started. John's entrance attracted gunfire and Luke's misplaced heroism gained him the loss of his sight.

Anita had stayed for the tale, originally listening from a corner of the room as she pretended to clean then just sitting down on the sofa completely rapt at the sad story. She wiped her tears and Luke felt her pity for him.

Joshua too was overcome with the tragic story. "Thank you for sharing that with me." I don't know if I'd ever be able to go to a bank again after that. He contemplated the heartbreaking events as he finished his coffee. "I have to get back to the gallery, Greg Newburg is coming to deliver some paintings and I want to handle them personally. Can Ted drive me back?"

"Sure. I'll see you tomorrow. Thanks for everything Joshua."

## 21

Anita chided Luke against going for walks in the park at night.

"It doesn't make a difference to me if its night or day Anita, the walk is the same."

"It's not you! It's the bad element that hang around that park at night! They're a bad sort of character. They see you getting out of your fancy car, they see you dress in expensive clothes, they won't think twice before beating you for any money you have." The plump housekeeper tried her hardest to talk him out of his plans.

"I know how to defend myself Anita, I'll be fine. I can do a great John Wayne impersonation, and scare anyone away. See you later." He certainly could scare anyone away he had once or twice bared his fangs for some thug about to take advantage of his apparent weakness.

Of course Anita was right about the people that walked the park at night. But Luke didn't care. Night air was different, Night people were different.

Suddenly he sensed a void that meant there was a vampire. He walked without thought toward the creature. He found a crumpled heap. A boy crying and hiding under a blanket which itself was under a bench.

"Boy, who are you? Why are you crying?"

The boy of maybe twelve or thirteen years old came out of his hiding place. "You're like the one that did this! You're like me! What are we? What did he do to me?" The child was understandably hysterical.

"Come with me, I'll tell you everything you need to know." He urged the boy to come with him and was at a loss for the right words.

"Get away!" He threw the blanket aside and ran

He was still just an infant as a vampire and Luke caught him easily. He carried the boy who fought him every step of the way. He was skinny and long, on the wrong side of a growth spurt that would have changed his appearance form child to young man. He threw him into the backseat of the waiting limo and ordered Ted to drive home in a voice that told the chauffer not to ask questions.

Once home he carried him easily up the stairs to the guest bedroom. "Calm down! I won't hurt you!"

The boy was obviously terrified. "Who are you? Please don't hurt me." He was sobbing now. "What am I?" He cowered in the corner of the room frentic with fear.

Luke decided the child needed to calm down. He took the boys hand and gently massaged it. He spoke soothing little phrases "shh, it okay, there there now" until finally after perhaps ten minutes the boy was quiet.

"What's your name?"

"Jimmy?" He answered as if it were a question.

"Jimmy, who did this to you?"

"There was a guy, all cool like Marlon Brando. I was following him. He went into the movies and I walked in after him. Next thing I know, I'm in the park. And I can see every little thing and I can hear people's hearts beating and I can smell them. They smell like blood. There was this bum, sleeping on a bench and I went right up to him and just bit him and drank his blood! It was really good, best thing I ever had! Man! Why didn't anyone ever tell me it was so good? I felt better than when I snuck my Dad's beer. I went home and my parents were dead. Oh my gosh! My parents!" He started sobbing all over again.

How sick! How sad, this poor kid had lost everything. He wished he could give him a drink or a pill to make him sleep but none of that would have any effect on him. After ten minutes he finally calmed a little.

Luke thought about asking Jimmy to try to sense the whereabouts of the mysterious vampire, but decided against it. Jimmy could barely handle the situation. It was too much for anyone.

"Go take a bath, then go to sleep. Listen don't be scared when you see blood on your face, it's the tears. Just go to sleep."

## 22

The next morning Luke called a department store and had clothes for Jimmy delivered to the house. He called the gallery and told Joshua about his visiting cousin. Then he set about to educating the boy for survival.

Jimmy didn't have any trouble learning his new skills. He also didn't seem to care about losing his humanity or his parents. Luke thought he was probably supressing it, unable to deal with the horror.


Anita was thrilled to have a boy in the house, even though she thought he was stand-offish and too rebellious for his own good. But so often these days kids his age were like that.

He took off without permission for long periods of time. Luke would find him most often in the movie theatre watching whatever was showing. Luke gave the boy too much spending money.


Luke often brought Jimmy to work with him. He could keep an eye on him and he could use lunch hours for lessons and the all-important nip and sip.

"It's more fun to kill them! Why can't we just drink it all. They don't matter!" Jimmy whined

"You have to respect people. You're going to live a very long life and if you can't respect people, you'll be very lonely. Why would you want to kill, if you don't have to? You're not a killer."

"Get with it." Jimmy left yet again. He never stayed around for conversation or confrontation.


Luke couldn't send him to school. He would be recognized. He hired a private tutor, a woman named Charlotte Fellows who met him each day at the gallery for his school work. Luke knew they didn't have long, after a year or so people would begin to question why Jimmy wasn't aging.

The rebellious child got a kick out running away from his lessons and going to the movies. He didn't care how many times he saw the same movie. He was obsessed with the actors and actresses. Sometimes though he would run through the city and no one would find him until he showed up at the house later.

As the months passed, it was clear to Luke that Jimmy was very manipulative. He put on a good show of humanity, but there was very little human emotion in him. He didn't seem to care about anything or anyone. Luke held on to hope that he was just supressing his emotions after the horrific ordeal of being turned and finding his parents murdered.

Most everyone believed him to be mischievous and rebellious, but it was a show.

Luke couldn't give up on the boy. He tried repeatedly to show him love. He tried to be like a father to him and kept hoping that eventually he would grieve his parents' death and recapture his lost emotions.

Luke brought Jimmy with him each week to the Children's Home and hoped he might connect with the orphans in sympathy. He was kind to the children but he didn't befriend any of them. The children were the only people Jimmy seemed to be kind to. He sat quietly listening to the stories Luke told, and helped out when help was needed.

Luke even went to the movies with Jimmy. They saw *The Day the Earth Stood Still, The African Queen, A Streetcar Named Desire* and countless others. Movies seemed like the only thing that Jimmy really liked.

They were watching *The Thing from Another World* when Luke sensed the other vampire in the theater.

When the vampire realized two others of his kind were in the theater he left quickly. Luke ordered Jimmy to stay and watch the movie, and left him. He seemed completely unaware of the other creature.

Luke caught up to the vampire not far from the cinema.

He chose to approach him with civility rather than conflict. "I'm Luke Logan, I don't believe we've met. I wasn't aware that there were any others of our kind in the area."

"Luke Logan." He said with disgust. "You pitiful fool. Don't you dare imply I don't have the right to be here!"

"I wasn't implying anything. I thought we might try some mutual courtesy. Obviously that isn't one of your abilities. What's your name?"

"I'm Julius. It's not your business but I'll be civil." He spoke with disdain.

"You turned a boy and left him, confused and terrified. Why would you do that?"

"What makes you think it was me? You're blind, this is a big city there are plenty of our kind here. It could've been anyone."

"Fine. I can't prove it, but I have a feeling I am much stronger than you could imagine. Don't test me. Stay away from the boy." He was barely civilized at this point. His anger was a caged tiger.

"I doubt that a blind vampire could ever beat even the weakest, much less me. Turning you should have been a crime. See you some other time." And he was gone.

Luke was still at a loss as to why he would do something like turn a boy into a vampire, and then leave him. He went back into the theater where Jimmy still watched the movie.

# 23

Jimmy was missing again. Mrs Fellows was beside herself with the unruly student. "I can't be expected to teach him anything, when every time I turn around he's gone!"

"I never blame you, he's a troubled boy with a tragic past. Please just have patience. I know it's hard."

"You pay well, and I need the job. So I'll stay. After my husband's accident I honestly didn't think I could find a job that would pay well enough to make up for his not being able to work. I need this job, so I'll stay. But please talk to your cousin."

"Yes ma'am." Luke left in search of the young vampire. He was frustrated beyond belief.

Luke had found Jimmy in the movie theater again. He slipped in by his side. He could smell human blood on the boy. Luke spoke quietly, too quietly for any human to hear him. "Jimmy, you are supposed to be with Mrs. Fellows."

"That's too bad. I don't need any more education." He said in a voice anyone could hear.

Luke stayed quiet. "You do need an education. Have you been drinking blood? You smell like you've been swimming in it."

Thankfully Jimmy chose to answer in a preternaturally inaudible voice "I can't always just be expected to live the way you do I can't live on 'sips'. I was hungry. I killed a guy on accident. I'm not sorry. I liked it."

Luke didn't know what to say. He sat silently by his side and while Jimmy watched the monster movie. When the movie ended, he took the boy back home.

At home Jimmy refused to eat the dinner Anita had cooked. He stomped up the stairs and sat sullenly in the bedroom. All though Luke couldn't hear Jimmy's thoughts or sense his feelings, he could feel a blank spot that meant Jimmy or at least a vampire was there. He kept his attention the blank spot while he apologized to Anita for the boy's rudeness.

## 24

Luke didn't really know what to do with Jimmy. He wasn't the happy eager boy Caleb had been. He was nothing like the orphans he knew. This boy had been though a horrible ordeal. It was of course going to leave him scarred. Luke didn't know whether to lean toward leniency or discipline. The boy was brooding and mean most of the time. And of course Luke wasn't his father. He had no right to discipline him, except that Jimmy needed a home and Luke could provide it.

Luke tried offering up fun ideas but nothing but the movie theater seemed to please him. He could sit in the theater for hours, watching the same film repeatedly or on weekends watching everything that was shown from opening to closing.

Luke held hopes close to his heart that Jimmy would brighten up and let Luke be his father figure.


Luke found stables in a town not far from San Francisco and decided to take Jimmy. Luke couldn't imagine someone not falling in love with the horses.
Jimmy went begrudgingly. That was fine with Luke as long as the boy went. The stables and riding trails were set on a large property that smelled of home to Luke. The guide, Vince showed Jimmy the horses and let the boy choose from four waiting steeds. Jimmy chose a large quarter horse. Luke had been here several times before and always chose the same paint horse with the unoriginal name of Paint. Her name aside, she was a fast and friendly horse.

Vince showed Jimmy how to mount the chestnut horse named Adonis. With Vince riding out in front of Jimmy, Luke stayed in the rear. The cool clear air was wonderful. Birds sung in trees. Water from a small brook bubbled along past rocks. Luke loved this. He wondered how Jimmy was enjoying it.

The guide had moved closer to Jimmy, giving him directions on how to tell the horse what to do and where to go. They reached a large open field with a choice of trails depending on the experience of the rider branching out on three sides of the expanse.

"Can I try running him? I'll stay right in the field and then come right back. I promise!" He sounded honestly cheerful and full of hope.

"Sure, if it's okay with your cousin. Mr. Logan he has done a great job so far. He has a natural skill with horses." Said the Vince

Luke was thrilled that Jimmy was enjoying this. "Yes, absolutely." Luke would have joined him in the run but decided for now to let him have this to himself. He would join in later if he thought Jimmy would enjoy a race.

Jimmy took off. Luke listened to the beautiful and familiar sound of the horse galloping. He listened in as Vince watched the boy and the horse. Vince thought that the child was troubled but horses make great therapy. He could see how happy Jimmy was. And that was nice to see.

Jimmy returned after ten minutes. He spoke more on the rest of the ride than Luke had heard him speak in a whole week, but almost all the talking was directed at Adonis. They reached the last field of the ride just before they would return the horses to the stables.

"Wanna race?" asked Luke.

"Sure!" answered Jimmy with excitement.
The two took off and though Luke could easily beat him, he held back just enough to come into the stable area moments after Jimmy.

"Wow! That was great! Can I bring Adonis to get a drink? Can I help you take the saddle off?" he sounded like a child on Christmas morning.

"That's fine with me" answered Vince. He showed Jimmy how to walk the horse to the trough and after the horse had had his fill, he showed him how to take him to the pasture and remove the saddle and other gear.

Jimmy was gentle and kind to the horse. This was a side of him Luke had never witnessed. He was hopeful for the first time since bringing Jimmy home, that maybe he could find a way to bond.

## 25

Once again the next day Jimmy had taken off from his lessons. Mrs Fellows was beside herself. "I just can't take this!"

"Please, Mrs Fellows, don't quit. I will work something out for you. I'll figure this out."

"I feel like I have no choice, I really do need this job. I just don't know what to do. He's the most troubled boy I have ever met. I am sorry to say, I think he's really beyond my help."

"I think you may be right. I'm going to find you some work to do, to earn the money I'm paying you. You won't have to worry about Jimmy anymore. He's not your problem. Why don't you make some written lessons that he can work on privately. Then he can learn and you don't have to worry about being responsible for him. He can learn here, and you can send the lessons from home."

"Mr Logan, I can do that! But I do think the boy needs more."

"I know he does. I will find him the help he needs. Thank you Mrs Fellows. Please go home and I'll go find Jimmy."

He sent his mind out in search of the Jimmy and soon found him in the same park where he'd originally found him. He went to the park with his supernatural speed.

Jimmy was under a tree with someone. The person's thoughts were fuzzy. Luke realized quickly that it was a woman in a trance. As Luke approached the thoughts faded to nothing as her life was sucked from her.

"What have you done?" Luke yelled. He grabbed Jimmy with fury and carried him against his will at unheard of speed to his house.

Once there, Luke's rage was still boiling over. He threw the boy across the room and was instantly reminded of Celeste's similar act. His rage died in shame. He picked the younger vampire up off the floor. "How could you do that?"

"I wanted to get a real meal, you expect me to live some sort of monk. I'm not doin' it." The unrepentant child spoke to Luke as if her were an idiot. "You can't make me like you. You're weak. I'm not and I'm free."

"If you want to live under my roof and under my protection, you won't kill again." Anytime Luke had imagined using the phrase 'under my roof' it had never ended with 'you won't kill again.'

"This is so nowhere." Jimmy said and he went to his room.


Jimmy didn't exactly bond with Luke over the horse riding. But he did let him tell him about his times at the Double Jay. He listened as Luke told him all about Bessie and how beautiful and strong she was. Bessie wasn't sweet to anyone but Luke. She had bitten several ranch hands. She waited for Luke to do all her care. After his accident, she had finally had to let others care for her. When Luke had recovered enough to go back to the stable she welcomed him back with a whinney and nuzzled him gently. She could somehow knew that he was now more vulnerable than he had been. Luke had sensed it in her. When he rode her now, she followed the other riders instead of expecting direction from Luke.

Once recovered, he went back to being the only one allowed to brush her and ride her. She let others do the saddling but threw anyone that tried to mount her. He wondered if after he left The Double Jay she ever warmed up to anyone else. He thought maybe she did. She had let Caleb feed her apples and other treats from time to time.

# 26

Jimmy got a job in the mornings at the stable. He helped to brush and groom the horses. He cleaned out the stables. He did any job the owners asked of him. He did it all with relish. They let him ride Adonis after he was done. They were even considering training him to be a guide. The Jimmy of the horse stable was very different from the Jimmy at home. Luke gave him this. He loved to see him happy.

Jimmy arrived home one afternoon after work. He walked in to find Anita scrubbing the floor with ferocity.
"Jimmy, you are tracking dirt all over the floor! Why don't you go up and bathe before dinner. Son, you smell like a horse!" said the exasperated housekeeper.
"Thank you!" Jimmy said thrilled at the compliment about his odor. He ignored the warning about tracking dirt which was expected on Anita's part anyway and headed up the stairs to bathe per her instructions. He was always just a little happier and more compliant after he'd been with the horses.
Luke laughed.
"Oh sometimes you are as bad as that boy! Two children in a big house and I get to clean up after you!"
"Anita, you know you love it." Luke said and walked back to the study.
Anita knew he was right. She loved working for him. She didn't mind cleaning up after him or even Jimmy. She was glad to see that at least occasionally he could have some brightness in his life.

# 27

The children were all gathered around Luke listening to a story about a mysterious Indian prince. Jimmy stood in a far corner of the room talking surreptitiously to an eleven year old girl.

Luke was the only one who could hear the quiet conversation. At first it had seemed innocent, just Jimmy being unusually friendly. But the conversation had moved from two sided 'what do you like' questions to one sided commands.

"You are happy and calm Sally. You want me to kiss you now and you are not going to fight it. Take me to the closet." Jimmy whispered all these things to the innocent child and her numbed mind was not at all alarmed as she led him to the hall closest and entered with him.

Luke abruptly ended the story and jumped up to stop Jimmy who was now in the closet with Sally. The delicious odor of blood was strong in the air. But Luke tripped over a confused child as he tried desperately to get to the closet.

He scrambled up and feared he wouldn't get to the closet in time. "Jimmy! Jimmy! I need you! Hurry!" he yelled it hoping that Jimmy might come. He finally reached the door as it opened and a furious Jimmy stepped out.

Luke knew the girl was still alive but very weak. Jimmy had not taken enough blood to kill her but certainly enough to cause her to be very weak for several days at least, like when Celeste had kept Luke sick before she changed him by drinking only a little of his blood.

Luke reached past Jimmy and picked the child up. "Sam, go get Mrs. Simms right away and tell her Sally is sick."

Very quietly he spoke to Jimmy. "You had better get every one of these kids to forget you were in the closet with her."

"What's wrong? Can't you do it yourself?" Jimmy turned away from Luke. It seemed like he was going to refuse but he immediately got the children's attention and told them that Sally had fainted while listening to the story.

Luke felt every child agree at the false memory. He decided Jimmy wouldn't be coming to the children's home anymore.

"How could you do that? These children are orphans! I thought you had a little compassion for them." Luke was livid.

"I was hungry! She's just another worthless human. She's a kid now, but she'll grow up. Besides, it's easier for me to kill a kid."

"You were going to kill her? Jimmy, killing is wrong. Why can't you understand that?"

"I don't get, why you don't get that eating is eating. These people are just food. You are ridiculous. I hate you, I hate everyone."

Jimmy ran off and Luke let him go. He didn't know if he could deal with the young vampire anymore. And really, was it his problem? No, but he couldn't just release him into the world to kill. If her were free to be the vampire he longed to be he would be very dangerous indeed.

Luke hung up the phone with the legal firm. Jimmy had been living with him for nine months now and Luke was preparing to send him to Sabatok until they could make further arrangements. He'd given him his own account with a healthy amount of money. He knew that under the guidance of the vampiric law firm the money would grow into a fortune soon enough. Jimmy would never have to worry about money.

Sabatok felt like he could really help Jimmy. Luke was happy to pass his student onto his teacher.

The next day a package arrived, holding identification papers and everything else Jimmy would need for his life. Jimmy was supposed to board a plane and meet Sabatok.

One hour after the package arrived. Jimmy and all his belongings were gone.

Luke felt like the dupe he'd been accused of being. He had held so much hope that Jimmy would improve, he'd believed his act. His heart was broken.

# 28

Luke stepped out of the car in front of the large house at The Double Jay Ranch. He stood in front of the house and took in his surroundings. The smells of cooking beef, grassy fields, horses, cattle, manure and hay mixed to form ambrosia. Luke breathed it in. People bustled about inside and outside the home.

No one form his past was alive anymore. Eli's grandson Gregg ran the ranch, which now boasted three large homes filled with family. Luke knew it wouldn't be the same but still The Double Jay was home and always would be.

Maybe Luke had hoped to reinvent Caleb in Jimmy. He had to mourn the boy somehow. He wasn't dead but Luke had lost all hope in Jimmy. He knew Caleb, Ike, Melba and Harvey were all gone now. Were they waiting with Melinda for him to join them? He never would. Even if her were killed his malevolent soul would never gain access to Heaven with them.

He considered leaving before anyone could notice him there. But of course a limo would be noticed quickly at the busy ranch. Before he could knock or turn and leave the front door was opened.

"May I help you?" a busy woman asked.

"Yes, I believe Mr Carter called to let you know I was coming. I'm Luke Jones representative for Logan Meats. I've come to tour the ranch and see that it still meets our standards. We hold our standards very high when it comes to where we procure our beef and even though you are our oldest and most trusted ranch, we still need to check in on you occasionally."

"Yes, Mr Jones, let me show you into the office and we'll get started soon. I'll find Mr Thomas."

The housekeeper or whoever she was led him to a large room down the hall to the same room that had been in his own office seventy plus years earlier. He ignored her thoughts so he could concentrate on the house, his beloved home. He still knew every inch of it.

The smells of furniture polish were different now and he knew the furniture wold not be the same. He could hear the hum of electricity, computers and phones. He let all those changes out of his mind and he stretched his mind through the house up the stairs and from room to room. To him it still looked the same. He could imagine Melba cooking in the kitchen, and although the smell of baking bread wasn't present his imagination placed the familiar loaf of freshly baked bread on the table right where it should be, waiting for him to steal his slice.

Mathew Thomas entered the office and spoke in a slightly too loud and nervous voice, "Mr Jones, I'm Mathew, the ranch manager and I'll be happy to take you on a tour. Let me know any questions I can answer for you. I assure you we hold to very high standards here."

The two got into a car and Luke was disappointed not to ride horses to see the vast property. He was taken to the horse pasture, current cattle pasture, and stables. Luke chose to walk as much as possible. But of course it was no longer his ranch, his land or his friends. It was Gregg's ranch now. He had hoped to meet Gregg but he was not present.

Luke left The Double Jay and knew he would never return. Caleb, Ike and Melba weren't there. His heart was with them not with the land or the structures. Jimmy hadn't broken his heart. Celeste had smashed it years before Jimmy had existed. She had stolen too much from him. He let his hope for Jimmy go to the same place as his sentimental longing for home.

# Part Three

# 1

Luke and Sabatok disembarked the private jet. Sabatok laughed his deep laugh and said "Well it looks like you have the power of flight."

"I've had the jet for years now Sabatok, you should visit more often."

Luke took out his smart phone and dialled his chauffer to make sure he was ready and to ensure the luggage would be transferred to the car.

"Sabatok I wish you would stay with me for a little longer."

"I can't. I have people expecting me. It was good to see you though. And I thoroughly enjoyed your jet."

"Good-bye old friend, I'll see you again soon."

They parted and Luke was met by his middle aged chauffer Martin who walked with him to the waiting limo.

Luke was on his way to one of his favorite homes. The large ranch style home was on a huge plot of land. Luke had stables now at all his houses. This house was just outside Dallas in Plano Texas. The house reminded him of The Double Jay without the family.

Once at the house he left his luggage up to the staff, changed his travelling clothes into the more comfortable jeans and t-shirt he preferred and headed out to the stable.

Mike was there waiting with Coffee, a strong, sweet and spirited horse. Her name didn't match her color. Luke had named her for her personality. Mike, who took care of the horses and the stables as well as the general land maintenance, had told Luke he couldn't name the Palomino, Coffee, it just wouldn't do. But Luke had been stubborn and hadn't bothered explaining his choice of name.

Luke mounted the horse and took off at a run. All his stress was left behind. He could feel the joy of the horse beneath him. He slowed her down and let her meander along as she chose. He stretched his mind out and felt the wonderful freedom of his privacy.

He breathed deeply of the clean air. The hot sun was warm on his skin. Birds tweeted above him. Small animals scurried along the ground and in the bushes hoping to go unnoticed by him.

When he felt that Coffee had rested enough and he felt her restlessness for another run, he said, "Home Coffee, let's go." He pulled his legs tight against her and she let go and ran. He let her go where she pleased and as fast as she chose until finally they got closer to the stable and house. He slowed her down for the benefit of those watching. He knew they trusted his horsemanship, but he doubted they would continue to trust it, if they witnessed the horse running at break-neck speed with her blind passenger barely holding the reigns.

Once in the house, Luke was greeted by Sheila, his head housekeeper who like so many of his housekeepers felt like she had to mother the very young man. She saw him as barely more than a child. She fully respected him but also felt it was part of the job to make sure he washed behind his ears and ate balanced meals. In this new century people his age were still considered kids. He had to accept that he was seen as a child regardless of his businesses, wealth or responsibilities. Of course disability added to what people saw as vulnerability. Regardless of how powerful he was. People would always see him weak.

"You need to eat your supper Luke, it's waiting for you. You sit in the dining room and Sven will serve it. I swear if I didn't make you eat, you'd just plum forget." She said in her charming southern accent.

Luke chuckled "you're right about that Sheila. Thanks."

# 2

At home Luke was well respected by his staff. At work, he was having a hard time finding that respect. He'd hired a woman name Merrill Fletcher to be his assistant at the gallery. She was an art history major in her fifties who had looked for the job after the youngest of her children left for college. She seemed incapable of remembering that Luke's opinions were the ones that counted at the gallery.

He appreciated her tastes and trusted most of what she liked. But she couldn't get past his blindness or his youth. To her his blindness equaled inadequacy. She made decisions without him and he often had to overturn those decisions in an effort to maintain his authority.

He'd only opened his Dallas gallery three months ago shortly after settling in Plano. He was trying to wait for her to get past her pity. He was patient, but he also wanted to enjoy coming to work every day and that was being hampered by the woman. He was beginning to see that it was more than pity and that she wasn't going to let go of her prejudice.

Evan Drummond came into the gallery right on time for his appointment. Merrill rushed the hopeful artist into Luke's office, and Luke followed behind. When he arrived only moments after the other two Merrill was sitting behind his desk.

"Merrill, you're in my seat." He said, then to Evan. "Mr. Drummond I'm so happy to meet you. Have you brought some of your work?"

"Yes Sir" said the polite young man. He was nervous and he had no idea how to show a blind man his paintings.

"Merrill, please go ask Abe to come in, thank you." Luke said to the woman.

While she was bringing the art teacher into the office, Luke explained that he would ask Abe, Merrill and Evan himself to describe the work. Those descriptions would give him a basic feeling for the painting and he would know whether or not it suited his gallery.

"It's real unusual to have a, um, visually impaired person interested in art especially enough to own a gallery. Your gallery is real nice too. I like all the art appreciation you do for the kids too."

Merrill entered the office without knocking and Abe followed behind. Luke heard the clicks of Abe turning on several lights so that he and Merrill could better see the work.

Evan had brought three pieces with him, oil paintings of space and with fantastical views of mystical planets, and vortexes. All three paintings evoked interesting emotion from the assistant and the teacher. There was a desire to explore, to move, to hope that there was something or someone out there among the lonely stars.

Merrill spoke, "We've never really hung science fiction kind of paintings, I don't know if they're right. I mean I like them and you're talented but your work might be better suited in another gallery. Let me get you a card for a gallery that does like your sort of work."

Luke pushed his frustration with the woman down so that he could remain pleasant to the now very disappointed artist. "Mr. Drummond. I like your work. It speaks to me. I like you and I want to offer you a show here. Do you have enough work for a show?"

"Yes sir! I have about thirty paintings at home."

"Great, let's plan the show for a month from now. Someone will be to your place to choose twenty paintings and make sure they are all as high quality as these. We set the prices; we keep 40% for what's sold in a private show, 30% in a group show and 25% for display. I'll have contracts ready for you on Tuesday."

"Thank you! Thank you Mr. Logan." The excited artist gathered his paintings and left, feeling he was finally on the verge of success.

"Ms. Fletcher, I need to talk to you privately"

Abe left the office quickly, since Luke's annoyance was evident.

Merrill was already angry and she felt irritation at Luke's acceptance of the work.

"Luke it was good work but really, space and fantasy are not our thing." She spoke to him as if her were to slow to understand and now she would be stuck with his mistakes.

"This is MY gallery. I've been in th s business a long time. I liked the paintings. I make the decisions here."

Merrill interrupted him. "You're barely what twenty five at the oldest? My kids are older than you. You can't have been in this business for a long time. You own this gallery because you inherited it from your rich daddy. You can't appreciate art. You need to leave the running of this company to me and go home and walk your dog."

The haughty woman had gone too far. Luke held is anger in check, but not too much. "I own this gallery I've done more in my lifetime than you can even imagine. I have climbed mountains, and run marathons. I buy and sell companies every day. I made myself who I am, not my Daddy, who by the way you never knew and have no right to talk about! I run this gallery. I will make every decision here until I decide to entrust it to someone else. You're not going to like my next decision. You're fired. Because you deserve more pity than I do, I'm going to give you a nice little severance package. You can leave now. I'll have your things delivered to you along with the severance package. My lawyer will bring them."

Merrill was stunned. She grabbed her purse and left the building in silent indignation.

Luke had enjoyed degrading her and he didn't like that about himself. He called the paper to put place an ad. He called Abe and asked him to step beyond his teaching duties and step in as his assistant until he could hire someone. Abe agreed, happy to be rid of the opinionated woman.

# 3

    Luke walked and scanned the minds around him. He searched for evil without thought for the reason. Deep down he knew that he was hungry for the blood bliss. But he didn't think about that he just walked, scanning minds, breathing deeply and hoping to calm down.

    There was a group of about fifty people gathered together. They were singing, and they all felt peaceful, happy and some even seemed beatific. He could feel that there was pain there too but pain with hope and peace in the mix. Luke was more than curious.

    Luke entered the open doors of the building. He was immediately greeted by a big middle aged man. "Welcome to Faith Community Church. We've just started the worship. You've only missed one song. Let me help you find a seat, Son." He then led Luke to a folding chair near several people all standing and singing.

    Luke didn't know any of the songs but they were all songs to God. They were like prayers in musical form, telling God He was wonderful, ensuring the petitioners that God would take care of them. The adoring singers emanated peace and joy. Luke stood with them listening to the songs and letting his empathy replace his feelings with those around him.

    After the singing everyone remained standing for a long and poetic prayer from the passionate man who had welcomed Luke to the church. Then the man spoke for some time, reading from the Bible and teaching his congregation that like James said it was no good just to tell your hungry naked brother "I hope you get food and clothes" you had to give your brother food and clothes.

Luke liked this philosophy and he wondered if they lived by it. He hated passing by the wealthy churches that left the poor and the hungry to beg.

After the teaching, the pastor led another prayer and a different man led one more song. Then the congregation started socializing. Many of them gathered around him, eager to introduce themselves and hear all about their visitor.

The pastor introduced himself as David Holmes. He was friendly and genuine. Luke sensed this man truly cared, and he actually listened to the answers from anyone he spoke to.

David explained that normally services were on Sunday mornings but this was the final night of a weeklong of services meant to be a revival for the small church.

"Please come again. Can you make it Sunday morning at 11:00?" Mrs. Holmes asked.

"I'll be here." Luke answered. 'Can you give me the address? I'll give it to my driver; I don't think he'd appreciate my directions to your church." Mrs. Holmes laughed and her son Kevin placed a business card in Luke's hand.


Sunday's service was similar to the Friday night service, but there were more people present. Luke felt very welcomed by everyone. Luke held back from the nip and sip amongst them, somehow it just felt wrong.

# 4

Monday morning had Luke busy scheduling interviews for Merrill's replacement and speaking to the law firm preparing her severance package.

That afternoon the three candidates for the job came in. Luke interviewed each first, and then had them tell him what they thought of the pieces in his gallery. He paid close attention now not only to their appreciation of the art but also to their attitudes regarding his disability and supposed age.

None of the three he saw that afternoon were right for the job and he scheduled three more for the next day.

Tuesday morning he met with a lawyer from the firm to approve and sign the severance package and gleefully sent her to Merrill's home. He had a paralegal with him for Evan's contract meeting. But Evan signed the contract without requesting any changes.

The lawyer reported to Luke that Merrill Fletcher had indeed accepted the severance and signed a contract stating she wouldn't sue the gallery or collect unemployment. There would be no need to collect unemployment when the package was a very generous year's salary.

"You're much too kind Mr. Logan." The lawyer said verbally but his thoughts said 'you're too weak. You should have fired her, let collect unemployment and compelled her, or you could have shown her how powerful you are and then killed her or compelled her.'

"Mr. Balding, I know you must be aware I can read your mind. I was kind to Ms. Fletcher by choice and because she is truly ignorant of my strength, even though she was blatantly disrespectful to me. You know what I am, and I could show you, in any number of creative ways that you'd be best off to respect me.

"Mr. Logan, I do apologize." He said insincerely. "You're right, I work for you, I should respect you. You might consider respecting the power that Constantine, Carter and LeRiche hold as well."

Threats exchanged and both parties feeling self-righteous, Mr. Balding left.

# 5

Luke's third interviewee Eliora Massey came into the gallery. Abe practically tripped over himself to welcome the beautiful woman. He was still thinking how pretty she was when he let Luke know his appointment was waiting.

She was serene. That was Luke's first impression of her. Luke approached her, hand out and introduced himself. "Hi, I'm Luke Logan, the owner here, please come to my office and we'll talk."

Her handshake was warm and secure. She followed him into his office. She was surprised that the owner was a blind man, pleased that he was young and handsome, and impressed by his gallery.

"Tell me about yourself Miss Massey."

"I graduated art school three years ago and I've been teaching art at a private Christian school. I do like the job, but I want to do more. I've always dreamed of discovering the next great artist. I just think there is so much undiscovered talent out there."

He liked her.

"Are you an artist?" He asked.

Oh no, not me. I'm much more an appreciator. I have a great eye." She paused a moment stumbling over her phrase but recovered and continued. "I can put things together to look amazing. I can spot true talent from insincere balderdash and I can design a display that shows off all the best qualities of a piece."

He already had decided he would probably hire her. He asked a few more questions and took her out into the gallery. "I want you to describe this sculpture to me, please."

She looked over the piece and collected her thoughts. He could feel her comprehension of the artist's talent, and her approval the work.

"It's very modern. It's metallic and smooth, very shiny, made up of rectangles and parallelograms connected at angles. It gives me the impression of movement. Like each rectangle is trying to take off from the ones beneath it. In whole it gives me the impression of a man with his hands reaching up to the heavens. Like he's about to fly."

"Miss Massey, You made me want to buy that piece. Can you start in the morning, say eleven?"

"Sure! Thanks. Call me Elli, please." she was jubilant now.

He gave her the paperwork to fill out and told her about the salary and benefits and sent her home. He had never before looked forward to working the next day as much as he did now. He had planned on having Abe train the new assistant but he decided he would take on the majority of her training.

# 6

Eliora fit into the gallery very well. Although Luke had hired a party planner for Evan's big show since it was too soon to give a brand new assistant the job. She worked alongside the man and made sure that Evan's pieces were displayed with great thought.

Luke discovered he liked her not only as his employee but also on a personal level.

He'd never much given into the cliché of asking what someone looked like. But his curiosity was stirred. Did she look as lovely as her personality implied? He knew Abe thought she was beautiful but Abe didn't spend time thinking phrases such as 'she has long blonde hair and a pointy nose', so he really only knew that she was attractive to nearly every man that walked into the gallery.

He thought about asking Kelly. Kelly was the new receptionist and all around 'do whatever we need guy.' He was a young, strong guy who had only last year graduated high school. He had an appreciation for art but no formal education. Abe had taken the young man under his wing, in hopes of encouraging the spark of talent he had noticed. But being so young and new he wasn't sure how far to trust him with the question.

Luke was talking to Henry Gamble a flamboyant photographer who insisted on be called Henri with a French pronunciation, and got annoyed that people kept forgetting. It was hard to remember a large and loud Texan wanted to be called Henri instead of the better fitting Henry. Henri didn't find Eliora to be particularly attractive although he had noted to himself that she was very pretty.

It didn't surprise Luke. He had long suspected but never cared that Henri would find Steve or Joe more attractive than any woman. Henri often thought about how good looking Luke was but he never acted on it or even thought further on it. So Luke didn't care. Most people never thought much of Henri's sexuality because although flamboyant he wasn't even a little effeminate.

"Henri," Luke said careful to address him with the French name. "This might seem like a strange thing, but, can you tell me what Eliora looks like?"

The big man laughed "Sure, I figured you like her. I'd bet everyone around here but Elli herself knows it."

Luke was going to protest, but decided not to bother. If everyone knew but Eliora then Luke was the second to the last person to come to this knowledge, but he couldn't help but know it was true now.

"She's about a head shorter than you, but you know that much probably. She's got real thick wavy light brown hair, kinda dark gold. Her face is pretty and round with hazel eyes. When she's real excited they're greener but mostly they're regular hazel. She doesn't wear much make up, just a little. She's curvy, not fat, not big breasted even, just kinda soft and round. If I liked women I'd like that figure, not skinny, not fat not top heavy. Don't you worry Luke, you didn't pick a dog."

"Thanks friend." Henri left the office and Luke sat back trying to picture Eliora.

# 7

Once everyone had arrived to work Luke gathered them for his announcement. He could feel the nervousness from nearly everyone. "I'm closing shop today. Anyone that wants to go to the beach, we're going."

Abe spoke up first. "Boss, the closest beach is about 7 hours drive from here and um, none of us is exactly dressed for the beach."

Luke could barely hold his excitement. "You may forget that I am filthy rich. If you want to go to the beach, go home pack an overnight bag, and meet me back here in an hour. We'll go to the airport from here and board my jet. I'll make sure we have all the extras you just bring bathing suits and clothes."

Kelly was brimming with anticipation. "What beach are we going to?"

"Any beach you want to go to! Let's do the whole weekend! Pack for three days."

"I've always wanted to see the ocean. Any beach would be great with me." Eliora was elated. This had been a dream for years. Her family had never quite managed the promised beach vacation.

"Well then let's do Malibu. See you in an hour at my place. Abe, Kelly bring your girls."


The group pulled up to the beach house which looked more like a beach mansion to Kelly. He had never seen a house like it before. It was modern with multiple levels, and square lines. Kelly wished he had a girlfriend to invite here but he had brought his buddy Tony. Tony was just as impressed.

The inside of the house was as sumptuous as the outside promised it would be. Luke stood still trying to get a feel for the house from everyone's thoughts and impressions while they explored the first floor. Abe was impressed with the large sunken living room and its overstuffed furniture and fire place. Kelly had immediately found the kitchen and was thinking how great it would be to cook a gourmet meal in it. Eliora had found the entire back wall of the great room slid open to a huge deck with stairs down to a private beach. She was chomping at the bit to get there. But she was also thinking of Luke. She realized he'd never been in this place before and he could use a little quiet help.

Eliora went to Luke and suggested they tour the house together first, then everyone could get changed and head out to the private beach. Luke decided he could definitely like this girl. She was sweet, thoughtful and appreciative.

There were three levels to the house. The upstairs had five bedrooms each with its own bathroom. It was obvious the house had been built especially to be used for vacations. The first floor boasted the huge sunken living room, a dining room, another bedroom, two more bathrooms, a theater room, and the huge kitchen. The downstairs had a huge game room, indoor hot tub, and another two bedrooms. All three levels had decks and beach access. There was another hot tub outside on the second level as well as a swimming pool and party deck.

The group stepped out onto the beach as one. Of all of them only Luke and Abe's girlfriend Shannon had ever been to the beach before. Luke enjoyed the awe the felt as they glimpsed the vast blue ocean for the first time. Kelly and Tony ran for the water like the children they were, and were already splashing one another by the time Abe and Shannon got there.

Eliora quietly put Luke's hand on her arm and walked to the water. "This is amazing. Thank you for giving this to us. What made you decide to do this?"

"I figured if I felt like I needed a vacation, maybe we all did." I like a little spontaneity sometimes. I feel like I have to have everything so planned out. This morning I decided I wanted to go to the beach. What's the use of having money if I can't let people enjoy it?"

"Are you really rich? I mean I know you have a lot of money, but are you really really rich? Is that rude to ask? It is, I know. But until today I didn't know you had a jet. I'm just a little surprised. You don't dress or act like I would expect someone would if they were super rich."

Luke laughed. There was no greed in her question. She was surprised and impressed. "I am filthy stinking rich beyond your imagination. My family owns Logan Meats as well as a few other things. I won't lie. I like a nice house. I have servants. I enjoy the luxuries. But I'm glad I don't dress or act rich. I hope I'm just me, not a snob, just me."

"You are you, and I think I'm going to enjoy getting to know you. But I thought that before I thought you were dripping money."

"I know you did Eliora."


While the group was enjoying the beach, and poor Kelly was getting sunburned, a private chef cooked a feast. Everyone came downstairs freshly showered and ate voraciously. The huge meal satisfied everyone but Luke.

The second night, Luke opened up the house to the beach and for a big party. Kelly and Tony had spent the day exploring the surrounding town, meeting neighbors and inviting everyone they saw to attend.

Eliora watched Luke mingle and flirt with the many party-goers. She felt just the slightest twinge of jealousy and couldn't decide why. Her hint of jealousy gave Luke a little joy.

# 8

Luke changed his children's home days to Saturday because he enjoyed spending Sundays with his church friends.

He still enjoyed the children's home visits but nowadays only the younger of the children cared to sit for his exciting stories. The older ones preferred video games and Facebook. And all of them preferred a movie to his yarns. So he had story time but also arranged field trips to the movies, the zoo (he let someone else show them the big cats), and even the occasional play. He had tried to take some of the older children to the symphony but all but one had been bored stiff. Kyle who had enjoyed the symphony was given season tickets to the next season so that he and a friend could enjoy the music.

Luke invited Eliora to church with him.

"Maybe sometime, Luke but I have a church I've been a member of since I was twelve years old. I really like it. Let me think about it or maybe you'd like to visit mine."

"Well, I love this church. I'm new to the whole church thing and I've never felt so much like I belong to something."

"I guess for now, we'll both just attend our own churches."

For now. For now implied that it could change. For now implied she thought there was more to their friendship than just the present. He wasn't just taking her words but her emotions and thoughts as well. He soared in happiness, when having a request denied might have left others dejected.

At church he found that his good deeds far outnumbered any of his friends. Of course, his bad deeds far outnumbered all of theirs put together. He wasn't prideful about his good deeds and he didn't holler about them either. He just did them.

The amount of money Luke gave away each year was much more than most men would make in a lifetime. Now Faith Community Church was among the happy recipients. He spent hours each week volunteering at various places.

He learned that God forgave your sins, if you asked. He would just wipe out all the bad deeds a person had done.

Luke asked Jesus to forgive him. He thought there was much too much to forgive but the church taught him that if he asked Jesus to forgive him he was forgiven, and now they told him he was a Christian.

It felt good to be a Christian. But he still felt guilty for his past. Pastor Holmes told Luke that it was hardest to learn to forgive yourself. You just had to live the best you could now.

Luke tried to be good, but he still wanted the blood. He took his nip and sip but he refrained from the members of his church and he refrained from Eliora. There was something about her she was light, she was pure, and he felt like stealing her blood would defile her, and he would feel cursed forever if he did that.

# 9

Eliora was going to visit an elderly widow, and invited Luke along. She had packed a casserole and a basket of books for Mrs. Henderson who loved to read. They were standing outside her apartment in the retirement community when Luke realized the woman had cats. He froze, trying to decide what he should do.

He had once before not been paying attention while walking in the park, and a feral cat had jump from a bush and attacked him. The cat had gone crazy scratching him and screeching loudly. Luke had been sure the cat wanted to kill him. He had managed to get hold of the feline and toss it away from him before he moved as quickly as humanly possible away from it. Now there were three of the creatures waiting on the other side of the door to attack.

"I need to tell you something. I'm allergic to cats" Luke said.

"I didn't realize, and she has three of them!" she paused thoughtfully. "How did you know she had cats?"

Luke laughed nervously "I'm like Daredevil! I can smell them. But seriously I depend a little more on my sense of smell than you do. Can't you smell the kitty litter? I can."

"Oh! Duh, I guess that makes sense. Well, let me go in first and ask her to put them away. She keeps a really clean house so I doubt there will be a lot of dander around. I can't smell kitty litter at all. Maybe you do have Daredevil's senses."

Eliora knocked on the door and entered, explained the problem and Mrs. Henderson put the cats in her bedroom.

Luke finally came in to the cozy apartment. The cats howled and hissed in the other room.

"Elli sweetheart it's so nice of you to visit. Who is your friend?"

"This is Luke. I work for him at The High Avenue Gallery. He's become a good friend." Eliora answered.

"Welcome. Sit down both of you. I've made a pot of tea, Elli, Dear do you mind pouring?"

"It's so nice to meet you Mrs. Henderson" Said Luke as he extended his hand.

A soft warm and wrinkled hand took his. "My pleasure. So exactly how close of friends are you?"

"Oh, Mrs. Henderson! You are too much!"

The cats were becoming louder, scratching, screeching, and trying desperately to get out of the room.

"I don't know what's got into them! I suppose they don't like being in the room but they normally don't mind." Mrs. Henderson was getting very upset for her beloved pets as well as for her guests.

Luke felt awful since only he knew the reason for the cats' behavior. "I am so sorry Eliora, Mrs. Henderson, I forgot I have an appointment and I really must be going. Eliora, I am going to take a taxi, please stay and finish your visit." He stood up and Eliora jumped up to guide him out of the apartment.

"Luke, do you really have to go? Can't you cancel?"

"No I can't. Sorry. I'll call you later." He left before she could protest further. He could feel she was baffled and a little angry.


An hour later his phone rang.

"Luke, what got into you? I do not believe for a second that you had an appointment. That was just plain rude. "

"Please forgive me Eliora." He begged. "I am more than allergic to cats and I wasn't well. They were getting to me. I freaked out. I'm sorry."

"You freaked out? Are you afraid of little kitty cats?" She was incredulous

"It's hard to explain. But just please understand and forgive me."

She couldn't stay mad at him. She had noticed he was a little quirky. So she put this up to that. "Fine, you're forgiven. I will not take you on any more visits to the widows unless I know for sure they don't have cats. Maybe I'll desensitize you and adopt a kitten for you."

Luke laughed, "Thank you, even though I know you can't understand it thank you. I'll pass on the kitten. Let's start with a plush toy if you really feel the need."

# 10

Christmas had been one of Luke's favorite times since he had long ago started his Christmas parties. This year was even better because He had his church friends and best of all he had Eliora.

Sheila had loved planning the party. This party was going to include a huge cook out with a whole cow (Which of course had been provided by Logan Meats) slow roasted on a spit. There would be every kind of food imaginable. Luke had hired a large staff just to cook and a larger one to serve. Sheila, Sven, and the rest of his staff would be at the party with him. They were all happy with the idea.

The evening of the party the smell of the roasting cow, made even Luke hungry. Twinkling lights decorated the inside of the house and hung in every tree outside. Luke had one gift for each person at the party. Even the children would receive only one gift each. They didn't have the same appreciation in the twenty first century that they had had in the nineteenth. A nineteenth century orphan had thought an orange was the best gift ever and a coat had been an unimaginable luxury. A twenty first century orphan would put an orange to the side looking for a real gift and be disappointed with a coat. He couldn't blame them. Not only were things more accessible now, they were expected to be happy with less, while more fortunate friends received expensive computers, phones, and game systems. So he got them each one gift, but he knew from searching their thoughts that it was one gift each child truly wanted.

Eliora arrived at the party, and saw Luke, not dressed in his usual jeans and cowboy boots but in an Armani Tuxedo. She had always thought he was handsome but she was stunned for a moment by his exquisiteness. He blushed at her admiration and hoped she didn't notice.

She went straight to him through the party goers to tell him hello. She hoped to spend the majority of her evening with him. That's good, thought Luke, because I want to spend it with her too.

"Luke, The place looks great! Everything looks great. You look great." She gushed.

"Eliora! Thanks ,I'm sure you look great too. I've been told by more than one person you're really beautiful. I bet your outer beauty almost lives up to your inner beauty."

"I think that is one of the best pick-up lines, I've ever heard. I keep telling you most people call me Elli."

"It's not a line, I mean it. And I think Eliora is a lovely and special name and you deserve to be called by a lovely and special name."

"Well then thank you."

Eliora stayed by Luke's side for the whole evening and for both of them this night marked the change from friendship to romance.

# 11

Luke and Eliora sat in a small Mexican restaurant. Eliora wanted to think of something fun to do. "Let's go see the circus!"

"No," Luke answered "I hate the way the animals are treated" He also couldn't help but imagine what a lion or tiger might do in his presence. "Not only that but it's sort of boring for me, I mean I can't see what's happening, you have to spend the whole time telling me. It's not like a movie where there's dialogue."

"Okay then, how about dance classes?"

"Dance classes? Seriously?" He asked hoping she was joking.

"Luke I've seen you dance, you're not all that good."

Luke gave her what he hoped was a sheepish grin, "I'll let you give me private lessons."

"Luke Logan!" she said as she smacked his thigh "Well then let's try, Karaoke!"

"I listen mostly to classical music, and I don't know all the words to any of the hits." Luke explained. He felt like he was just shooting everything down.

"Oh that's okay," she said with hope, "they show the words on a little TV monitor. You just read them."

Luke laughed "Well Eliora if they have them in braille I'll give it a shot. We can go and I'll listen to you sing."

"Oh, Sweetie, I'm sorry, I just wasn't thinking. No to Karaoke. How about the Drive-in movie?"

"Now that is a good idea. I like that one. You pick the movie."

The next evening Eliora picked Luke up in her small and old Toyota Celica and they drove to the drive-in which was showing old B horror movies. Luke loved the idea of the drive in because they could talk as much as they wanted and not bother anyone. The movie that was showing was *The Thing From Another World.* Luke couldn't help but think back to Jimmy.

Eliora ordered a ton of junk food. The movie started and as it played Eliora gave commentary where she thought it might be needed. Eventually she and Luke were only barely watching the film as they talked about other things.

"I didn't know you listened to classical music. You always struck me as a country music fan." She said honestly.

"I used to go to the symphony and the opera a lot! I never liked the clothes I was forced to wear to that stuff but I but I did like the music. I have a sound system at my house that plays music in any room and it sounds great. I almost always have it playing in the background at home. Sheila doesn't like it, she tries to change it out for fifties music. I let her sometimes. What kind of music do you like?"

Eliora thought about it. "I like worship music, instrumentals and I guess I'm sort of a fuddy duddy but I like the stuff they call 'adult contemporary pop' like Josh Groban and Andrea Bocelli. Do you know them? I think you'd like it.

"You'll have to let me listen sometime. I really don't keep up with what's new. I'm an old soul in a young body."

The movie ended and Eliora drove Luke home and declined his invitation to come inside.

# 12

It had been nearly a year since Luke had last found himself in this position. He was in a penthouse apartment, a rich, greedy despicable, and dead man lay bloodless at his feet. Luke breathed hard as he enjoyed the ecstasy of the blood.

When it finally left him he bent down and lifted the dead man in his arms and laid him on the bed. His shame overwhelmed him and he cried for several minutes. "Oh God! I'm so sorry I couldn't help it! I don't want to do this. Please take this bloodlust away! Please God forgive me"

Then he washed his face and finished his disgusting job. He put the man's gun in his hand poured whiskey all over the bed, lit a cigarette and threw a lighted match into a pile of whiskey soaked clothes. He hoped that the body would be too burned to figure out it was bloodless. He didn't care if it looked like murder, as long as they didn't question that it was supernatural.

But as Sabatok had always said, people saw what they chose to and believed what they needed to. He had found that true. He knew that there had been rare times someone not meant to see his fangs had seen them, but completely ignored the fact.

Vampire myth was so popular now that people might connect a bloodless corpse with vampirism, but still they would choose to believe that it was a person masquerading as a vampire or a person with a bizarre fetish.

His shame followed him home. He called Eliora and talked with her. She could tell something was bothering him.

"I don't feel like talking about it. It's just guilt over something."

"Guilt never helped anyone. Whatever it is, if you've been forgiven, you've been forgiven."

# 13

Whenever Luke had dated in the past it had been all about what he wanted to do and what we would enjoy, now he wanted to find things that would please Eliora. He picked her up in the limo, and instead of champagne, he had her favorite drink, diet mountain dew ready for her in champagne flutes. They drove out to White Rock Lake, Luke told Ted to relax and return when he called. He took the picnic dinner and blanket out of the trunk and walked with Eliora to a spot she chose.

Luke served her favorite food. Cheese burgers, and chili fries. Eliora was thrilled with the surprise date. Luke checked his watch. It was just about time. "I brought you here to see the sunset. I've heard this is the most beautiful spot in Dallas to watch the sun set."

"Luke, thank you. It's amazing. I love sunsets. Did I ever tell you that? I don't think I ever did. This is the perfect date, my favorite food, my favorite time of day, and my favorite person. It couldn't get any better."

Luke didn't ask her to describe the view but her natural compassion led her to describe it anyway. He couldn't recall ever seeing such a beautiful sight in his life.

After the sun was down, and her dinner was through, Luke pulled out two red velvet cupcakes.

"Another of my favorites! How did you know?"

"It's my goal to know what you love and what you want and give it to you. I love you Eliora. I really do."

She leaned in close to him and her warm lips were on his. It was a soft gentle sweet kiss. It was the first kiss in many many years that he hadn't even considered taking a sip. He enjoyed it through his entire body.

There were a few more kisses on the ride home but Eliora made him feel like the sweet little kisses were all he needed from her.

# 14

Eliora was arranging some new brass sculptures with Luke standing nearby 'looking' at them for himself. They were a series of faces with a mask three inches in front of the face. The face and mask each held different expression. From straight ahead a person would see a smiling girl but come closer and move to the side and the viewer sees there is a mask, come closer and you see the girl beneath the mask is furious.

Luke thought they were great. He considered buying the serene mask hiding the plotting man. He hadn't decided yet.

"Can you hand me the sculpture you're touching please, Luke." Eliora asked.

Luke held the mask out toward her. She took it from him and their hands touched. He felt her elation at the slight touch along with his own.

"Luke, I'd like to go to lunch today. Kelly can handle the gallery while we're gone.

"Lunch sounds great. What are you in the mood for?"

"I'd love some barbecue."

One of the many things Luke enjoyed about Eliora was her down to earth honesty. Most other women would have chosen a fancy trendy expensive meal, but Eliora chose what she liked and wanted. She didn't bother with the 'oh anything is fine.' stuff either. He asked, she answered. He could kiss her right here. But she preferred their public affection to be hand holding and the like.

At lunch, he could tell she had something on her mind, but he allowed her thoughts to be her own. He knew she would share what she wanted to, when she wanted to. He could choose to read a person's thoughts at will, but his empathy had no on or off switch. She was happy but with a reservation.

Finally she said, "I need to talk to you about something important. But I think it should be in private."

"Come over tonight"

"You have too much staff at your place, I only ever go there, cause I know we won't be alone."

"Then come over tomorrow and we'll go horseback riding and have a picnic. We can talk about anything you need to."

"Okay." She had a flutter of nervousness and then relief.


Eliora rode Cami. She was a multicolored Appaloosa, so named by Mike because she reminded him of camouflage.

Luke, of course rode, Coffee. They walked the horses for the most part but as they neared the gazebo in the middle of the wild flower covered field they raced the mares to the finish line. Luke let Eliora win.

They dismounted and unpacked the picnic Sheila had made for them. Finally Eliora took a deep breath and spoke what had been on her mind.

"Luke, you are the kindest, most giving man I have ever met. I've never met anyone as accomplished and yet humble. But," she took another deep breath. "I think you're hiding some secret from me and from everyone. I think you should be able to tell me anything. I want you to know whatever it is, I love you. I won't stop."

Luke could tell there was more, but this was plenty for now. He took some deep breaths.

"I do have a secret. I'm so ashamed of it. I don't know if I can tell anyone. I don't think anyone could keep loving me, if they knew."

"I love you Luke. God loves you. Nothing can change either of those two facts. God's love for you is perfect and unconditional. Nothing you do can make Him love you more or less. He loves you more than you could possibly imagine. He already knows every bad thing you've done. He loves you anyway. Me, I love you so much, it hurts sometimes. I love you more every day. You don't have to be afraid of losing me."

"I'm evil, the worst of the worst. God can't possibly love me, and I don't deserve your love."

"I wish you could understand God loves you anyway. What is it you've done that is so evil?"

Luke tried to think how to put this in human terms so as not to break his vampiric oath.

"I have an addiction. Please don't ask to what. I can't tell you, for my safety and yours."

"You're in danger? You put me in danger?"

"You're not in danger! I would never let anything happen to you. I just can't tell you about the addiction. It's horrible. I go months without it, then I give in without even thinking. It makes me do horrible things. No matter how much good I do, or how much money I give away, I can't make up for all the repulsive evil I've done."

"Sweetheart, I'm so sorry." She squeezed his hand

"I'm sorry. I try so hard to be good. But it overcomes me. I need it. I try not to, but then I give in."

"God still loves you. I still love you. You don't have to be stuck like that. Nobody is good without God. No amount of good deeds can ever pay the price to cover even the smallest sin."

"Then it's hopeless. I may as well drink and drink and not bother trying to get on His good side."

"It may seem hopeless. God only has a good side. The only way to Him, is through Christ. Christ was the only one who could pay the price, and when He did that, He paid it for all of us, all we have to do is believe it and accept it."

"I believe in Jesus. I belong to a church. I do a lot of good." Luke said

"Luke you can't just believe in Jesus, you have to believe that He is God come to earth, that He lived a perfect life, He never sinned. Do you know everyone else is born a sinner, but not Jesus, and even though he was tempted by Satan himself, He still didn't give in to it, even once. He died a horrific death. Three days later God resurrected Him, He overcame death and that is what allows us to be forgiven of our sins. When we ask God to forgive our sins, when we tell him we believe what Jesus did for us, and we give ourselves to Him, it changes us. You can't simply believe in Jesus you have to simply believe in his life, death and resurrection and accept the gift of His redemption."

"Let me think about it, I don't think I understand it. I've done horrible things. I don't think it can be as simple as you say it is."

# 15

Sunday at church, Luke wanted to ask David about what Eliora had said, but he couldn't bring himself to ask. These people all thought he was a Christian like they were. He had even thought so himself until yesterday. There had to be more to it, than just believing a few facts.

David read from the Bible "I'm reading from The Message 1 Timothy 1:14-19

> 'I'm so grateful to Christ Jesus for making me adequate to do this work. He went out on a limb, you know, in trusting me with this ministry. The only credentials I brought to it were invective and witch hunts and arrogance. But I was treated mercifully because I didn't know what I was doing—didn't know Who I was doing it against! Grace mixed with faith and love poured over me and into me. And all because of Jesus. Here's a word you can take to heart and depend on: Jesus Christ came into the world to save sinners. I'm proof—Public Sinner Number One—of someone who could never have made it apart from sheer mercy. And now he shows me off—evidence of his endless patience—to those who are right on the edge of trusting him forever.
> Deep honor and bright glory
> to the King of All Time—
> One God, Immortal, Invisible,
> ever and always. Oh, yes!

I'm passing this work on to you, my son Timothy. The prophetic word that was directed to you prepared us for this. All those prayers are coming together now so you will do this well, fearless in your struggle, keeping a firm grip on your faith and on yourself. After all, this is a fight we're in.'"

He went on to speak about sharing the good news of God's mercy with people and about remaining faithful. Luke barely listened. His mind was on Paul, who he knew to be considered one of the greatest Christians of all time, if not THE greatest Christian of all time. Yet, he called himself "Public Sinner Number One"

After the service Luke found David and asked "What did Paul mean when he said he was public sinner number one?"

David was surprised by the question, he'd thought Luke had known more about the Bible but he was happy to teach him. "Well before Paul met Jesus, he was a high official in the Jewish religion. He had a special hate for Christians, he tortured and killed many himself."

"Really? And God forgave him?"

"Of course, He did. No one could do anything that God couldn't forgive, Luke."

"But Paul made up for it, He devoted his whole life to serve God."

"Paul did devote his life to serving God, but not to make up for it, none of us can do anything to make things up to God. He did it out of gratitude and love for God. We do good things for God as a natural extension of our faith in Him, not because we have to do good things to earn our way."

"Thank you David." Luke left, contemplating everything he had learned.

# 16

Sheila read Luke his mail every day. She held the fancy invitation in her hand. "Dear Mr. Luke Logan, The Altruist Society of Greater Dallas has named you Man of the year and requests your attendance at a ball in your honor. We wish to present you with an award noting the great good you have done to benefit the people of The Greater Dallas area."

"Mr. Logan, how wonderful!"

"Sheila please do me a favor and decline. Try to get it mailed off in the morning so that they can choose some other person." He knew he wasn't deserving of the honor and he preferred to keep a low profile.

"Oh, Mr. Logan, it's a real honor and it would be a fun night for you. I doubt most people know half the good things you do."

"I don't need people to know the good things I do, and I don't need them to pat me on the back. I'll write a letter telling them that I decline the honor but I'd love to attend while they honor someone else. How's that?" He doubted anyone would find him truly altruistic if they knew how truly atrocious he was. But he didn't care about recognition.

"You confound me young man. You dictate the letter to me, it'll be faster that way. I'll mail it first thing in the morning."

"Thank you Sheila."

The party was held at a ritzy downtown hotel. People arrived in limos wearing expensive clothes and more expensive jewels. Luke noted that none of the less fortunate that these supposed altruists supported were here. The only benefit he saw to the party was that guests paid an exorbitant fee and that all the money went to the charity of the honoree's choosing.

They were honoring a woman who had started a company to help female ex-convicts move forward to life outside prison. She helped them find scholarships for college, good and safe housing, counseling and other services. Luke thought it was a good charity and wrote a large check for donation.

Eliora and Luke danced often and ate the rich dinner. Luke spitefully took more than his required nip and sips as he made the social rounds at the party. He was actually a little buzzed at one point and had to be careful not to alert Eliora to his condition. But she simply thought that like her, he was having a wonderful time.

The party reminded Luke of his evenings with Sabatok. He should have invited him to come along. Sabatok would have loved the rich blood that attended the party.

# 17

Luke and Eliora sat together at the Gazebo talking.

"There has to be more to this than what you're saying. How can one man's death mean that I can be forgiven?" Luke had been struggling with these questions and Eliora had patiently been answering. It reminded Luke of his times with Sabatok guiding him in the vampiric gift, which had cost him so much.

"Jesus is more than just a man. He is God, and He is the Son of God. He gave up his Godhood and came to earth as a man. But because God was His father, He was born without sin. He lived his entire life without sinning, even once. He never lied, or stole or even had a bad thought."

"Okay, well, how does his good life affect mine? I try to follow his example, but I can't do it. I sin all the time. Everyone does.

"You're right. We all do. The Bible tells us in Romans 3:23 'For all have sinned and fall short of the glory of God.'

"That means we can't live up to God's hope for us. And Romans 6:23 says' For the wages of sin is death, but the free gift of God is eternal life in Christ Jesus our Lord'.

"So when we sin, and we all have, the only way to pay for it is by death. But Jesus didn't owe his life, because he had never sinned. So he died in our place."

"1 Peter 2:24 puts it like this He himself bore our sins in his body on the tree, that we might die to sin and live to righteousness. By his wounds you have been healed.'

"Jesus took every sin you ever committed or ever will commit and put it on himself. He took the blame, he paid the price. He was tortured for it. And He died, and paid the price."

Luke interrupted; I still don't see why one death can be equal to billions of deaths."

Eliora held his hands, she loved him so much, and even his questions made her love him more. She wanted him to understand this and accept it.

"If he had just died, then that wouldn't be enough. But three days after he died God resurrected him from the dead. God brought him back to life again by The Holy Spirit, who is the third part and person of God. The fact that he overcame death, and that's what gives his one death the power to overcome billions. We're all going to be resurrected one day. Some of us will live forever with God, and some will be separated from him forever in torture."

"That's heavy stuff" said Luke sounding like a hippie, but he was sincerely thinking about everything."

"So you say all I have to do is just believe that and accept this gift of happy forever?"

"All you have to do is believe it, accept it and follow Christ, but before the happy forever, there's life here. He never promised a rose garden. He just promised to be with us through our suffering. Luke, I know you think you've sinned more than anyone else. I know you think you've done unforgivable things, but you can turn your back on all that, you can ask for forgiveness, and God will forgive you. He's just waiting for you to ask."

"Thanks Eliora, and thanks for being so understanding that I need time to understand all this."

# 18

The gallery party was going full throttle. People went from exhibit to exhibit eating miniature foods and drinking expensive wine. Four artists were sharing a show. Eliora was talking to a couple about a large painting. The wife wanted to purchase it, but the husband wasn't so sure. Eliora was speaking to the man's ego in an attempt to get him to buy. She was very good at her job. Before long the man decided he needed the painting and he bought it as a gift for his wife.

Luke was a wallflower, listening in on the party goers. He waited impatiently for her Eliora to be finished so he could spend a little time with her. She was a better employee than he wanted her to be and she spent the entire evening working. As soon as the last of the guests left, Luke found Eliora took her by the arm and escorted her outside. "Lock up please! Thanks!" He shouted to whoever would be closing. He didn't care and he trusted that it would be done.

"Eliora, do you trust me to be able to take care of you?" Luke asked.

"Yes, of course I do." She answered.

"Okay then let's just walk, I know it's late but I love to walk." Luke felt her trust in him, her lack of fear because he was by her side.

She cuddled in close to him and the two walked together without care for where they were going.

"Tell me about your childhood Eliora."

"My child hood was a suburban dream. I was the only child of parents that had me when they were a little older. My Dad was a doctor and my mom was a nurse. When my mom decided it was time for a child, she gave up her career and had me. They spoiled me. They gave me everything I could ever want. It was really a very happy childhood. I don't have lots of hidden tragedy like so many people do. My family was happy. I was well adjusted. I made good grades in school. The sad part came after childhood. My parents died in a car accident driving to my college graduation. I found out about it after the ceremony. It was horrible losing them both that way."

"I'm so sorry." Luke said. He could feel the pain renewed. He felt her resolve and her strength grow larger around the pain too.

"I was lucky to have them. They were really wonderful."

They walked silently and comfortably for a few minutes.

"Tell me about your childhood."

"Well, mine was pretty great too. But not tragedy free, still no life is. I was born and raised on a ranch. My Dad was a really great guy. He raised my brother and me to take over the business. It was great being a kid on a ranch. I loved the horses. I would sneak into the pasture every chance I got and ride. The ranch hands looked the other way. I was like a little prince, spoiled rotten by everyone on the ranch. John, my older brother was the good one. He never would have gotten into trouble if it hadn't been for me. I would get caught for doing whatever bad thing I had done that day and he would take the blame for me if he could. He got spanked for stealing more cookies and breaking more lamps..." he was quiet for a few moments as he thought of his brother.

"Mom died when I was seven. She and John had been very close. She counted on him for everything after she got sick. He was old enough to understand that she was dying and take on all this responsibility. He never complained. They were so much alike, quiet and strong. He even looked like her. When she died he got really withdrawn for a while. He was thirteen. I turned to our housekeeper Melba. She was wonderful and she took over mothering me and John. I still got into all the same mischief but Melba didn't let John take the blame. Well anyway, I grew up loving the ranch. John died in a bank robbery. Did I tell you about that? I was blinded, but he died. I was seventeen when my Dad was killed in the war and suddenly I was rich, owned my own ranch, and I was really young."

Luke was quiet again, he had already told her one lie about John's death now he had to figure out how to move the story on without revealing any secrets or telling anymore lies. He hated lying to her.

"Yada Yada Yada I decided to move to Texas and open a gallery."

Eliora laughed. "That Yada Yada must cover a multitude of sins my Dear. But I'll let it go."

"Thanks."

"I guess that's why I always think of cowboys when I see you. You are a cowboy."

"I sure am. I've wrangled, I've wrassled and I've even dealt with my share of rustlers." He said in a western drawl.

# 19

Luke was in the mall. He'd found it an interesting place to do his version of people watching and he was considering opening a second gallery here. He sensed the other vampire near the multi-plex cinema among the popcorn scented teen agers. The void had Jimmy's familiarity.

"Jimmy?" he called out.

A boy's voice answered "I'll catch y'all later my cousin found me and I guess I should talk to him. I'll text ya later." Jimmy headed over to Luke

"I was gonna look you up, I knew you were here, it's why I came. I've been curious about you."

Jimmy was so nonchalant as if it had been a week rather than nearly sixty years.

"Jimmy, are you Okay?"

"Obviously."

Luke was at a loss for what to say here. He had loved this boy like a son, he still did. But Jimmy had hurt him, and he'd become ruthless. He'd kept track of him for a couple of years through the Firm and they would coldly report that Jimmy killed nearly every night. Finally Luke was so sickened by it he stopped keeping track of his former student.

"I just want you to know, that I forgive you. It's not your fault, you were turned so young and you never developed your own morals. I love you Jimmy, I'm sorry that this happened to you."

"You forgive me? You are a pathetic excuse for a v-...man.! I was curious to see if you're still as pathetic. Besides I'm out of money. Give me some more."

"How could you have spent everything I already gave you? I'll give you some, only this once. Ask the lawyers to teach you to invest it because I won't give you more. I pity you Jimmy, that you never learned to love, that you are stuck forever looking like a child and that you only know selfishness."

"Don't pity me! You hypocrite! I've seen the real you, Killer! You better pay me something or else." and he was gone.

Luke loved Jimmy regardless of his countless iniquities. Luke did pity him. His condition made it so that he didn't understand that killing, or treating people like food was wrong. Even his fury was understandable when looked at through the eyes of pity. Luke was sad for the wretched little creature.

If he, a worthless murderer could love Jimmy, who wasn't Luke's creation, like that, how much more could perfect God love him who was His own creation? It was a revelation that elated Luke. God really did love him. God had created him, and understood he would come up short, because he wasn't perfect like God! If he could have flown, he would have.

He called the law firm and had them transfer one million dollars to Jimmy with orders to ensure that it was invested rather than wasted. He also made sure that only one hundred thousand would be released annually for five years, so the money could grow to last the endless life the boy might have to survive.

Two days later Jimmy was at Luke's front door. "I want more money! How dare you give me a piddly little allowance like you're my dad?"

Luke pulled the vicious vampire inside, down to the basement where no curious housekeepers would hear his rant.

"That is more money than you need to live, you'll be fine." Luke said trying to keep his anger in check.

"Are you kidding? You have more money that you'll ever need! I want more! I'll go to your pathetic little girlfriend and tell her what you are. She'll never want to be near you again. No better yet, I'll turn her!"

Luke let out a low growl. He spoke slowly still trying not to lose his temper. "Do not touch any of my friends. Do not make me promise what I'll do to you!"

Jimmy punched Luke hard in the face.

Luke spoke through a broken quickly healing nose. "You may think you're stronger than I am, but I promise you I am much stronger than you can imagine. Leave, don't make me hurt you."

Jimmy growled and hit Luke again then picked him up to throw him across the room. But Luke broke Jimmies grasp and held the vampire in front of him, like a toddler throwing a tantrum. "I can hurt you Jimmy; I have the power of the blood of the most ancient vampire. That blood, and my age make me very very strong. You might kill more than I do but you are still only a child in vampire years in a child's body. Don't make me hurt you. Please Jimmy. I love you. I don't want to hurt you."

Jimmy kicked and flailed uselessly while Luke continued to hold the howling creature.

"Fine, I have to do this, I have to show you, since you won't listen. Luke took one hand and held Jimmy by the throat. He still hung in front of him, he still kept trying to kick and hit. Luke squeezed, just a little. Jimmy couldn't howl anymore.

"Stop, please." Said Luke. He was calm now as he just felt sorry for the ridiculous child. "I don't want to hurt you but I will if you don't stop."

Jimmy gave the kicking more effort. Luke squeezed harder.

"If I squeeze any harder, you'll lose consciousness. Stop or I'll break your legs." Luke said the brutal words with the tone of a father speaking to a toddler.

Jimmy didn't stop, so Luke used his free hand and effortlessly cracked the boy's thigh bones, then dropped him to the ground.

"Now, I'm going to tell you to leave my house and never return. I will not swear to you what I will do, but I will remind you that right now, I could easily kill you and I choose not to do it. Fear me. Respect me. Leave."

Jimmy screamed against his will as his legs and the tender muscles of his neck healed. He scurried away crying with an unsolicited promise that sealed his fate. "I'll leave you alone I swear. I'll never bother you again!"

He left and Luke felt spent. Physically of course he was fine, but his emotions were drained. He walked up the stairs passed his curious housekeepers and walked silently upstairs, where he took a bath and contemplated everything.

He could see himself kicking God and God begging him to accept his mercy, the way he had begged Jimmy to accept his mercy. But Jimmy had been unwilling and Luke knew he'd be back when he forgot his fear.

Luke should have been respectful of God's power all this time. God could have killed him a million times over for his countless sins. Even before he'd been turned he'd been arrogant of God, assuming he was a crutch for weaker souls like Melba, when she, in fact had been strong and loving.

"Oh Lord! I've been so wrong. I completely ignored your love and your power. I took life. I lived like you didn't matter. I tried to make up for my sins without you. I am so sorry. I'm so thankful that you took it all on yourself. Please forgive me God. I'll follow you forever. I'll live for you forever. Thank you Lord! Amen!"

Luke wasn't aware of the seizure that followed or the frantic knocking at the door. He aroused as he was placed onto a stretcher and loaded into an ambulance. He felt strange. He passed out again.

# 20

He woke up and tried to decide where he was. Sounds were all muted, there was a quiet steady beeping, the hum of a fluorescent light and muffled voices on the other side of a door. He couldn't understand what was wrong with his ears. He stretched his mind but it went no further than the confines of his skull. He was confused. He realized he was very groggy and tried to fight his way to alertness.

He managed to move his hand and felt the tube coming from his other arm. And the wires attached to his chest and arms. Then he heard her sweet voice. Eliora was by his side "Sweetheart, it's Okay relax. You're in the hospital."

"What happened?" He couldn't hear her heartbeat or her thoughts. Her emotions were only conveyed to him by her voice and her touch. He felt as if he'd been blinded all over again. He had only known she was there when she spoke. This was bizarre. He suddenly and quietly realized he was a human. He wanted to jump for joy but he was not quite strong enough.

"You were in the bathtub, unconscious, there was blood in the tub and all over your face. They think you had a seizure but they don't know why. Thank God, Sheila found you. You could've drowned! Do you remember anything? Did you hit your head or something?"

"I don't remember hitting my head or having a seizure." He had to tell her. He had to let her know the best, the most important part of what had happened. "But just before that happened, whatever it was, I gave my life to Christ! I get it!"

"Oh Darling! I love you! I love you! Praise God!"

"I finally got everything you've been telling me. It fell into place. I was so broken, I felt so horrible for ignoring God all these years. I gave it all to Him, I gave me to Him."

Luke's stomach growled, and Luke realized he was hungry, not for blood but for food. He hadn't been hungry in about one hundred and forty years. "I'd like a nice big steak and a baked potato."

"Luke I think you'll be lucky to get chicken broth and Jell-O. You just woke up after sixteen hours unconscious.

She was spot on about his menu, but the next day he proved he could eat and did very well.

He knew he didn't have diminished hearing or smell. He had perfectly fine hearing for any human. He had somehow been cured. Edgar had gotten it right. There was a cure and the church had it.

Luke laughed.

"Are you okay sir?" said a concerned nurse.

"Oh yeah, I had questions for years and it turns out that the bumper stickers were right."

"What do you mean?" She asked worried that maybe he had a concussion after all.

"Jesus is the answer! I searched and searched and the whole time it was Jesus blood that I should have been looking for."

The nervous nurse wrote something on his chart and said "You get some rest now Mr. Logan." Then she rushed out of the room.

After three days of studies, they couldn't find any reason for what had happened and they could find nothing wrong with the vital young man. The hospital released him.

# 21

Luke was so happy to be home. Sheila was even happier to have him there. "Luke you look wonderful! Better than I have ever seen you look. Whatever it was that happened to you, it healed you from something. You look more alive than I have ever seen you. We were so scared for you. We opened the door and you were in the tub jerking around it was terrifying. Do you mind hearing it? I don't have to tell you."

"No, please, go ahead." He was curious and it didn't bother him. He was too happy about the results."

"Well, I had seen you storm up the steps. I knew you were really upset about something. While you were in the tub, I was making you some chamomile tea to help you relax. I went upstairs to see how long you were going to be and I could hear this splashing and like a gurgling sound. I screamed for Sven and I was banging on the door calling your name but you didn't answer. Sven reminded me I had a key and I used it. We opened the door and you were gurgling and jerking, there was blood in the water and all over your face. I was so scared for you. Sven called 911 and I grabbed hold of you. We got you out of the tub and eventually you stopped the seizure and you were just lying there so cold and still. Luke, I thought you were going to die, and I felt like I was losing my own son. I'm so glad you're Okay."

"Thanks, Sheila. I'm more than Okay. I really am."

Luke received a call from Constantine, Carter and LeRiche the day he got home from the hospital. "This is Mr. Constantine, Mr. Logan. I just want you to know that we are aware of your circumstances. I would like to assure you we have other human clients and will be happy to continue our services for you. Of course now we'll assist you with a more normal will." He paused to laugh at his own joke and continued in his strange accent. "This is a rare occurrence, any vampires whom you once shared a bond, will have thought the broken bond meant your death."

Luke thought of poor Sabatok imagining his death and mourning for him. "You knew that this could happen? You've known there's a cure and never told anyone?"

"It is not in my best interest to tell people about Christ. I work for the other side. If a vampire were to seek Christ with the purpose of a 'cure' as you put it, then they wouldn't find it. If one is seeking a cure then is he truly seeking Christ? It's rare that a vampire could humble himself to hear about Christ isn't it, and then humble himself further to accept Him? You see it has happened, but very rarely. Unlike you, most vampires enjoy the power they hold. Don't you miss the power?"

"No, I don't, and I don't miss the craving or the killing or the other weakness. I don't miss having to never love, and move every few years so no one will know what I am. No Mr. Constantine I don't miss it at all."

'Hmmm, interesting, maybe in time you will, or maybe you will relish your life the way few do, because you are aware that not everyone can have the gifts of true love or growing old. Well, Thank you, if you need us don't hesitate to call." The connection was closed and Luke hung up the phone.

# 22

In many ways, Luke felt like he had when he had first gone blind. He hadn't realized how strongly he depended on his empathy or vampiric senses to move through the world. He blamed his new clumsiness as he relearned how to be blind on his past addiction.

He learned to really use the white cane. He learned to listen to the sounds as they bounced off objects around him to say they were there. He practiced walking as much as possible around the house and the property, before he finally felt brave enough to try walking alone in the big bad world again.

Eliora was thrilled to see him no longer addicted to whatever the substance had been. She told him repeatedly how proud she was of him.

Going back to work he was more aware of his missing empathy. He still loved the art. He listened to the descriptions with a deeper appreciation now and trusted the tone of voice and words of the speaker now because he chose to trust them.

But God had given him other gifts as well. The Holy Spirit inside him had immense power, and although in his Christian infancy he trusted that power was there as he learned about it. He could sense whether a person was lying and more. It was like the Spirit whispered to him, Luke listened to that and obeyed. He learned much later this was the gift of discernment and he developed it as he used it.

He didn't miss the dark gifts he had paid for so dearly. He had much better gifts that Christ had paid for with His blood.

## 23

Eliora rode Cami a little ahead of Luke on Coffee. The two rode along to the gazebo. Once there Eliora was completely surprised and thrilled to find a picnic set for two. They dismounted and Eliora led Luke to the table. He waited for her to sit then he sat down next to her.

"Eliora, I love you very much. You have so patiently waited for me to become the person you knew I was meant to become. You loved me when I didn't know I was lovable. Thank you. I have to tell you some things that I need you to know."

Eliora listened as Luke told her about Melinda. He told her that he couldn't tell her everything or explain everything due to an oath he had made. But he told her about John dying in the war with his father. That it was really Melinda, his wife that had died that day in the bank. "I'm so sorry I lied to you. It was and is this oath. It makes it impossible to tell you the whole truth. But if I could, I would tell you everything. I just want you to know that not everything is seen. There is a supernatural world too and not everyone is human. I wasn't, but I am now, because of your love. If you can forgive me, I want to spend the rest of my life with you. I want to grow old with you."

"I don't completely understand. I trust God. He gave you to me. I am so glad you had Melinda. I'm so sorry you lost her. I forgive you and I would love to spend the rest of my life with you but, I would appreciate a proper proposal."

"I don't deserve you." Luke said as he got down on one knee and faced the most beautiful soul he had ever met. He held a small velvet box open to reveal a diamond ring to her. "Eliora, will you marry me?"

"Yes, of course, I will."

Six months later the house was decorated and packed with a plethora of flowers. The sweet perfume filled every room and met Luke as he and Eliora entered the wedding reception.

Their friends exploded in happy applause as the DJ announced the entrance of Mr. and Mrs. Luke Logan. Luke took his wife with a practiced flair and spun her to the dance floor.

As they held one another close, Eliora whispered to him. "I've never been so happy.'

Luke held her tightly "Me too. I didn't even know I could be this happy. I promise that every day I will strive to make you even happier than this. I love you." Tears of joy ran down his face. Eliora kissed them away.

## Epilogue

Jimmy crouched outside the bedroom in a tree and watched Luke's beautiful wife nurse her baby. Luke stood in the doorway of the room completely blind to him. He watched their easy conversation with longing. The baby finished nursing and the woman stood up fixed her robe and carried the baby to Luke. She placed the tiny bundle into his waiting arms and Luke cooed to the loved child. He bent his head down and kissed the baby's forehead.

Jealousy ripped through Jimmy along with the insatiable thirst. He reached to open the window.

Sabatok grabbed Jimmy before he could touch the glass.

Alarmed, Eliora thought she something at the window and instinctively stepped closer to her husband and daughter, but nothing was there.

Sabatok flew with the flailing weak vampire in his arms until he reached a high Tibetan mountain peak. In the middle of winter the peak was empty except for the lost corpses of the failed expeditioners. Sabatok dropped the foolish child into the snow. "I could make this very slow and painful if I chose. But, I'll choose the same mercy that Luke chose. Then in what he considered a very kind move, Sabatok ripped Jimmy's head from his body. He tossed it down with preternatural precision to a snow leopard far away and watched his natural enemy devour his unnatural enemy.

Sabatok was happy for Luke, he watched his friend enjoying his life. He even considered seeking the same answers as his friend had sought. Growing old with a soul mate looked very inviting.